Sky Allen is hesitant to love again . . . but why?

"Chet's a great guy," Dale said. Leaning closer for effect, he whispered, "You could do worse, y'know."

Smiling, Sky pulled her straw in and out of the opening in the cup's lid. *Hee haw*, it protested, *hee haw*.

"Go ahead, you and your soda can laugh if you want, but the truth is, Chet's one of the most respected men in Montana. I think you two would make a right handsome couple."

Sky frowned. "Cut it out, Dale. You know what I always say. 'Nothing ventured—' "

"'Nothing lost,' " he finished, rolling his eyes. "That motto of yours is getting a mite boring, if you don't mind my saying so. Your daddy, Wade, has been dead ten years now, Sky. You can't live in the past forever. And Wade would whoop your britches if he knew you'd been trying." He paused, giving his advice a moment to sink in. "You know I'm right."

LOREE LOUGH is a wife and mother of two daughters who makes her home in Ellicott City, Maryland. Her debut title, *Pocketful of Love*, was voted favorite contemporary (1994) by **Heartsong Presents** readers.

Books by Loree Lough

HEARTSONG PRESENTS
HP86—Pocketful of Love
HP151—Follow the Leader
HP157—Pocketful of Promises

Montana
Sky

Loree Lough

Heartsong Presents

To my family, whose love and support
is wider than the Montana sky.

A note from the Author:
*I love to hear from my readers! You may write to me at
the following address:*   **Loree Lough
Author Relations
P.O. Box 719
Uhrichsville, OH 44683**

ISBN 1-55748-805-3

MONTANA SKY

Cover illustration by Gary Maria.

prologue

Sky sensed the crosshairs of the sniper's rifle centered between her eyebrows and she crouched behind a boulder, one arm protectively encircling her Irish setter's neck. The last rifle shot, so recent that the scent of powder still hung in the air, had killed the she-wolf instantly. The dead wolf's life-blood slowly seeped onto the parched earth beneath her as two identical cubs trembled in the open space between the carcass and Sky's refuge.

Sky estimated the twins to be ten to twelve weeks old; weaned, but far from old enough to survive alone in the wilderness. Even they seemed to understand that cruel fact as they whimpered pathetically, nudging and pawing at their mother's lifeless body. Their mournful whining escalated as they learned about one of life's hardest lessons—death.

Too many times, Sky had been a student of that same cruel teacher. She recognized the sorrow that burned in their round, golden eyes.

Pebbles cascaded down the rock face and Sky knew it meant that the gunman was repositioning himself up there, searching for the angle that would guarantee a successful triple kill and add thousands of dollars to his bank account. What the cubs needed more than anything else right now was time. Time to find their pack. Time to plead for the acceptance of some other mother wolf who might teach them the lessons so vital to life in this beautiful yet brutal wilderness. Time to practice skills that would protect them from beast and nature and the most dangerous enemy of all, man. But for weeks, headlines had screamed, "Wolf Wars Rage between Animal Activists and Ranchers." Time was the one thing the cubs didn't have.

She looked into those sad, innocent eyes and swallowed hard. Chances of another she-wolf adopting them were slim, at best. And without a mother to protect them from pack hierarchy, they'd be outcasts, subject to slow, vicious deaths. Even the sniper's way was gentler than that. But it didn't have to be an either/or remedy. Her heart pounded as she made a potentially life-threatening decision.

"Hey, little guys, it's gonna be all right," she said softly. "I won't let anything happen to you. I promise."

Heads cocked and ears pricked forward, the wolf cubs froze, stunned into silence by their first direct encounter with the human voice.

one

The unmistakable crack of gunfire shattered the quiet, end-of-summer morning, and the bullet stopped with a sickening *thoomp* in the bark of a nearby tree. The wolf cubs cowered near their mother's dead body, yelping. Without a moment's hesitation, Sky dumped out her backpack, grabbed one yowling cub, then the other, stuffed them into the bag, and zipped it up, ignoring their terrified, confused cries. "Face, c'mere! Down, girl!" she ordered. Ears flat against her head, the dog, unaccustomed to such harshness in her mistress' voice, immediately did as she was told.

Cringing, Sky hunkered down behind the boulder, put on the backpack so that it rested against her chest, and secured its stabilizing strap across her lower back. The warm bodies of the cubs squirmed near her heart as she began what was as near a belly crawl as her front load allowed. Beside her, Face mimicked her movements. "'The Lord upholdeth all that fall, and raiseth up all those that be bowed down,'" she whispered, quoting Psalm 145:14. Sky sent a silent prayer of thanks heavenward to her father, Wade, for making her memorize Bible verses. "Never know when one will comfort or give you hope," he had said.

Another bullet zinged past, creating a tiny cloud of dust as it embedded itself in the rocks beside them.

Sky crawled faster. She knew it was no accident that the marksman had missed again; in these parts, being able to hit what you aimed at sometimes meant the difference between life and death. Murdering her was not his goal; her dead body wasn't worth thousands of dollars to him. She understood that the gunman's second and third shots were to scare her off so he could finish the job, unwitnessed, and exchange soft warm wolf bodies for cold hard cash. Just yesterday, *The Messenger's* front page had read, "Rumored Wolf Bounties Reach Record Heights." Montana authorities had taken a hard line, threatening steep fines and jail time for anyone caught trading wolf skins for dollars.

Well-worn buckskin gloves protected her hands, but the elbows of her flannel shirt and the knees of her jeans were torn and bloodied by the time she reached her pickup. Oblivious to the cuts and scrapes, Sky reached up and opened the driver's door. Face didn't need an invitation, and immediately leaped into the cab. The backpack still pressing against her chest, she drove like a maniac down Route 212, glancing every few seconds in the rear view mirror.

On the other side of the windshield she noticed the leftover glow of the moon, hanging high in the Montana morning sky, and she marvelled at the perfection of the natural beauty that God has created. She found it hard to believe that the celestial view harbored a cold-blooded killer.

It seemed to take hours to drive the six winding miles home from the foothills. One last peek in the rear view mirror satisfied her that no one had followed. For the moment, at least, she and the cubs were safe. Sky gave the steering wheel a hard jerk left, the tires creating a twenty-foot-long wave of grit as she turned onto the narrow driveway that connected her home with the rest of the world.

She removed the backpack and put it gently on the floor. Then slowly, so she wouldn't catch their wooly fur in the zipper's teeth, Sky opened the backpack. Yawning, the cubs poked their pointy noses through the opening and sniffed their new surroundings. The shooter's vantage point had provided him numerous benefits, including the element of surprise but now, Sky had an advantage of her own. During the Frightening Fifties, as Gramps had dubbed them, her grandfather had built a bomb shelter. Disguised as a toolshed, he'd equipped the underground room with every modern convenience. Virtually soundproof, it would be the perfect hiding place for her cubs.

The time that the cubs had spent pressed against her must have speeded their acquaintanceship, for they boldly stepped out of the bag. Side by side, the pair sniffed out the perimeter of the shelter, and christened each corner with a small yellow puddle.

"Going to need a lot of newspapers down here," Sky said, holding her nose, "and there's not a moment to lose."

Her watch beeped: Seven o'clock. In two hours, Lisa would arrive to assist Sky in neutering a calico cat. In the meantime, there was a lot to do to make the shelter a proper temporary home for the little wolves.

Sky made four trips between the house and the shelter, her arms loaded with things that would ease their adjustment to their new lifestyle. Worn-out quilts, piled in the far corner, would serve as their bed. An old clock radio, set to an "oldies but goodies" station, would play soft melodies to soothe them when she couldn't be there. She replaced the harsh white ceiling bulb with a yellow bug light that cast a warm, comforting glow. After feeding them a hearty meal of milk-softened dog chow, she filled a bucket with clean drinking water and left to resume life as the small-town vet.

Though it was cool in the operating room, Sky perspired behind her sterile mask. Deft hands efficiently and precisely handled scalpels and clamps as she mentally reviewed her decision to ready the cubs for their return to the wild. She knew precisely the level of commitment required to prepare them for freedom, because during her internship at the Atlanta Zoo, she'd worked with three wolf cubs discovered by University of Georgia students who'd gone hiking in Alaska. She and two other veterinary students assisted Dr. Williams. This time, since complete secrecy was the only way Sky could guarantee the cubs' safety, she'd bear the responsibility alone.

When her workday ended, Sky sat on the shelter floor, quietly inviting the cubs to come to her, knowing that to teach the cubs to fend for themselves in the wild, they must transfer dependence on their mother to dependence on her. Side by side, they sat on the thick old quilt, keeping a wary eye on her. Sky talked a lot…to Face…to the cubs…to God. The sooner the cubs grew accustomed to the sound of her voice, the sooner they'd associate it with food and comfort. But, much to Sky's dismay, neither cub came near her.

At the end of that frightening, frustrating, fascinating day, Sky slept the hard deep sleep of the exhausted. She woke before the alarm buzzed at five. Instantly wide awake and feeling like a child who'd received a puppy in her Christmas stocking, she dressed hurriedly and headed for the shelter, balancing a mug of coffee on the hard-backed journal she'd use to track the cubs' progress. They didn't cower when she entered the room. Rather, the cubs stood on all fours, heads low, and eyes staring, as she poured food and water into stainless steel bowls. Sky refused to step aside once their meal had been prepared and with her voice gentle but stern, she said, "Because this is the way things are gonna be from here on out." For several moments, the pair blinked round golden eyes and licked their lips. By five-thirty, they'd edged forward, one cautious step at a time, to eat their moist breakfast.

Sky yearned to tousle their thick, soft fur, to hug their fuzzy necks, to pat their flat little heads. "All in good time," she said, taking her affections out on Face, who greedily ate up the attention.

"When I get back," she said, pulling the door shut, "you guys are going to get some proper names. What do you think of that?"

Doggy brows rose and ears pricked forward as their heads cocked in response to her question. Their expressions made it hard to leave; she wanted to stoop down and gather them up in a big, rough hug. "Let's go to town," she told Face, locking the cubs into the safe solitude of the shelter, "and get those pups some real food."

Face understood the word "town" and because she loved riding in the truck, she bounded toward it at top speed, her high-pitched, excited bark leading the way.

"Patience," Sky told the dog, "is obviously one virtue you don't possess."

❧

When Martha Peebles' 1957 red Cadillac rolled up in front of The Grainery at eight o'clock, Sky had been waiting on the old green porch swing for fifteen minutes. "G'mornin'," her old friend said. "Aren't you the early bird!"

Sky grinned. "Twenty years ago someone wise told me that the path of a sluggard is thorny but the path of someone who is industrious is level and easy to walk."

The hoarse sound of Martha's laughter tickled Sky's ears, just as it always had. "Wise, you say?" the old woman said. "It's common sense and nothin' more."

Inside, as Sky piled the items on her list onto the long, red-flecked Formica counter, Martha gossiped. If it had been any other way, Sky would have to say she hadn't been there at all.

Half an hour later, Sky was paying for her supplies when a blue-jeaned cowboy slipped up and playfully tugged a lock of her hair.

"Well, I'll be," he said. "If it ain't Sky Allen."

Sky turned and met the clear blue eyes of her childhood friend. "Dale Rivers," she warned teasingly, returning his friendly grin, "you'd better have your running shoes laced up real tight if you plan to do that again."

He cocked back his black Stetson and laughed. "Shoo-eee," he tooted. "Just what I like…a woman with spunk." With that, he reached out and tweaked her cheek.

Sky responded to his playfulness as she had since both she and Dale were four years old, and put on a false show of fury. "I'll thank you to keep your mitts to yourself, cowboy!" she scolded, faking a frown to hide her grin and wagging her finger under his nose.

"You're still as cute as all get-out when you're riled." But the next time Dale reached for her, a large tanned hand clamped around his wrist and stopped it in midair.

"I think your hat must be too tight, Rivers," said a gravelly male voice, "and it's affecting more than your hearing."

His grin still intact, Dale said, "Relax, Chet. Sky knows I was just funnin'."

Sky glared, for real this time, as her so-called white knight droned on, "Can't you see the little lady wants to be left alone?"

"Little lady" indeed! Sky hadn't needed a man…for anything…since her father, Wade, had been killed nearly ten years ago. For an unblinking moment, she stared at Chet Cozart, owner of Four Aces Ranch—and Dale's boss. She'd heard a lot about him in the six weeks she'd been back in Mountain Gate, but this was her first face-to-face glimpse of the former rodeo star.

Crossing her arms over her chest, she inventoried her self-professed hero. Jet black hair, sun-bronzed skin, and rainy-day gray eyes that silently, broodingly said, "I know what's best for you." She'd seen that look before, and knew it would be pointless to tell the big lummox that she'd dealt with Dale's tom-foolery every summer day of her young life. In no mood to start a scene, Sky turned on her heel and stomped away without so much as a howdy-doo.

"Chet! What's got into you?" she heard Dale say as she reached the door. "Sky's been like a sister to me since we were knee-high to gophers. Why—"

"Well," the gruff confident voice interrupted, "try to mind your manners from here on out."

Sky slammed The Grainery's door, clenched her teeth, and headed for the skid, loaded with her supplies, that Martha's son, Joe, had parked beside her truck. "'Can't you see the little lady wants to be left alone?'" she ranted, mocking his drawl. Sky tossed ten cases of canned dog food onto the truck, one right after the other, picturing him all the while. Jeans that hugged muscular thighs, a cuffed white shirt that exposed beefy forearms, dark-lashed, glittering gray eyes....

Dale's happy-go-lucky words interrupted her reverie. "You've been in town nearly two months and haven't made time for your old buddy. You want folks to think you're still mad about that nickname?"

It said Lottie Marie Allen on her birth certificate but, thanks to Dale, everybody called her Sky. It all started the summer they turned ten, when Sky met a grizzly cub in the woods. Their game of hide-and-seek ended when the mama bear appeared and treed Sky. If it hadn't been for Dale, banging a soup ladle on a pot bottom, Sky believed she might still be up that tree. "Bet you can touch the sky," he'd teased after his drumming had scared off the bear. "Think I'll call you 'Sky High Lottie' from now on." Before her feet ever touched ground, he'd abbreviated it to just plain "Sky," a name that stuck like glue.

Sky filed the sweet memory away and stepped into Dale's outstretched arms. The decision to return to Mountain Gate hadn't been an easy one. She'd put off looking up old friends, afraid and uncertain about the memories each might conjure. "I've been awfully busy, setting up the clinic," she explained, backing out of his hug to study his friendly face. "Besides, since when do you need an invitation?"

Grinning, he glanced at his watch. "Shoo-eee! I'd better get a move on before Chet fires me and you end up supporting my sorry self." He dropped a brotherly kiss on her cheek and, walking backward, added, "Tell ya what. I'll pick you up at five. We'll go to our favorite restaurant. My treat." With that, he disappeared into the cowboy crowd.

Sky hopped up onto her truck's tailgate to rearrange supplies on the truckbed. Mentally, she listed Mountain Gate's eateries: The Silver Bullet Diner and Big Jim's Beef-o-Rama.

As kids, she and Dale and Ella spent a lot of time at Big Jim's. The summer they turned twelve, the trio started a business called "Anything for a Buck." Side by side, they shoveled manure, mowed lawns, babysat kids and dogs and even a goldfish or two, and then spent every penny of their earnings on Big Jim's burgers and fries. She was still smiling to herself when she noticed his reflection in her truck's rear window.

Oh, no, she thought, *Dale's back for more fun and games.* In the mirrorlike glass, she watched his arm rise and reach for her. *Well,* she added, grinning mischievously, *if the big goof thinks I'm gonna let him tug my hair again, he's got another think coming!*

She only meant to slap his hand away. Instead, the back of her hand connected with his eyebrow and sent him sprawling. Her father always said she was strong as an ox. "Don't know your own strength," he'd tease in a perfect Bullwinkle imitation. She blamed her vantage point, high on the truck's tailgate for the power behind the hit. Sky started to tell him she hadn't intended to hit him so hard, but stopped short when she saw that it wasn't Dale, but her self-named rescuer who blinked up at her. Chet had looked powerful and intimidating in The Grainery. Now, sitting there in the dust, he seemed small and vulnerable, and the sight tweaked a maternal chord in Sky's heart. "I'm sorry," she said. "Really. I never meant to...."

Sky jumped back onto the ground, landing squarely on both feet. She shook her hand and feigned pain. Grinning, she said, "That's some hard head you've got there."

Sitting up, he touched his already reddening left brow, a slow grin slanting his thick dark mustache.

Hands on hips, she said, "If you hadn't snuck up on me...."

"...And if you hadn't been up on that tailgate...." His grin broadened.

She smiled. "Guess I did have the upper hand...."

The handsome cowboy laughed. "You pack quite a wallop ...for a woman."

Ignoring his sexist reference, Sky stuck out her hand to help him up. Taking it, he unfolded all his six-foot-three body.

"No hard feelings?" she asked.

"Naw." He brushed street grime from the seat of his jeans as she lifted the last bag of cedar chips from the skid. "But if you'da popped Rivers this way in there," he suggested, gesturing toward the store, "maybe I wouldn't have felt obliged to protect your honor."

The sack hit the truckbed harder than she'd intended, splitting the bag and scattering sweet-smelling wood curls across the truckbed. His tone, the way he casually leaned against her fender, that smart-alecky lift of his slightly swollen left brow….

"If you'd bothered to ask," she snapped, dark eyes flashing, "I'd have told you my honor doesn't need protecting."

His right forefinger drew a small circle in the air. Sky thought for a moment he was about to point it at her before diving into some kind of male chauvinist lecture. Instead, he touched his swollen brow, winced, and pushed his black cowboy hat to the back of his head. "Don't I know it…now."

Stubbornly, Sky stretched to her full five-foot-nine-inch height and set her jaw. *If it's a staring contest he wants,* she decided, *I aim to win it.* To her relief, he blinked and looked away first.

He held out his hand. "Name's Chet Cozart."

"Sky Allen," she said, pumping his arm.

The casual get-acquainted touch became a crackling connection that sizzled between gloved palms and traveled on an invisible current that fused brown eyes to gray. "Guess I'll see you around," he said, releasing her hand. He turned, as if to head back to The Grainery, but abruptly faced her again. "What do you need with all that dog food? Your dog here," he said, patting Face's head, "is as slim as a dime."

Face nuzzled his gloved hand. When he bent down to pet her, she slurped his chin.

Heart pounding, Sky licked her lips. Had *he* been the man with the rifle? Did he already know why she'd purchased so much dog food? "Maybe you haven't heard, but I'm a veterinarian."

The mustache slanted again in a cocky smirk. "So I heard. What's one thing got to do with the other?"

Those clear gray eyes seemed friendly…inviting, even…and just intimidating enough to be the eyes of a sharpshooter. Even if he had nothing to do with the she-wolf's death, silence was still her best plan of action. "I can't very well let my patients starve while they're with me, can I?"

His slightly swollen left brow arched as he considered her answer. Then, tilting his hat low on his forehead, Chet saluted. "If you say so," he said, grinning as he walked away. "Have a nice day, now, y'hear?"

She teetered between fear and fury until she noticed his limp and wondered what horrible accident had marred his otherwise perfect physique. She slammed the truck's tailgate shut, grabbed the rusty metal skid's handle, and rolled it beside The Grainery's steps. *Martha will know what happened to him,* she thought, *and as soon as I ask her a few well-timed questions, so will I.*

two

That evening, over burgers and fries at Big Jim's, Sky told Dale about her second meeting with Chet, calling it "The Grainery Fiasco."

"Chet's a great guy," Dale said. Leaning closer for effect, he whispered, "You could do worse, y'know."

Smiling, Sky pulled her straw in and out of the opening in the cup's lid. *Hee haw,* it protested, *hee haw.*

"Go ahead, you and your soda can laugh if you want, but the truth is, Chet's one of the most respected men in Montana. I think you two would make a right handsome couple."

Sky frowned. "Cut it out, Dale. You know what I always say. 'Nothing ventured—' "

"'Nothing lost,'" he finished, rolling his eyes. "That motto of yours is getting a mite boring, if you don't mind my saying so. Your daddy, Wade, has been dead ten years now, Sky. You can't live in the past forever. And Wade would whoop your britches if he knew you'd been trying." He paused, giving his advice a moment to sink in. "You know I'm right."

Pouting, she tried to knot a french fry. Her mother had run off and left them before Sky turned five; by the time she was fifteen, both her beloved grandparents had passed away. And her dad's death, two days before her seventeenth birthday, left Sky without a family. The solitary lifestyle had prompted her to rewrite the cliché, "Nothing ventured, nothing gained," to be "Nothing ventured, nothing lost."

Dale shook his head. "I think it's mighty sad, that's all. You're a great gal, and you deserve to be happy."

Popping the knotted fry into her mouth, she looked up quickly. "What makes you think I'm not!"

His blue eyes glowed with the warmth that can come only from years of friendship. "You can't kid a kidder." Then, wiggling his blond brows, he began counting on his fingers, "You're both bullheaded, tall as trees, love animals, adore kids, *available*...."

Winking, he said, "You're perfect for each other."

❧

Long after Dale brought her home, Sky sat on her front porch, relaxed by the knowledge that she'd accomplished a great deal during her long hard day. Sipping lemonade while relaxing in Gramps' old rocker, she remembered Dale's "Chet praises" and smiled. His insistence that she get better acquainted with his boss puzzled her, since Dale had never been much of a matchmaker. His boss. His rich, know-it-all boss.

Martha had told Sky that Bud Houghton still lived at Four Aces Ranch, even though the property now legally belonged to Chet. And rumor had it that Bud, not Chet, had initiated the hefty bounty that had cowboys all over the territory lining up wolves in their gunsights. But it stood to reason that if Bud hated wolves that much, so did Chet. *Birds of a feather, and all that,* she thought. *And this bird,* she decided, recalling the scene at The Grainery, *is a genuine peacock.*

Actually, Sky thought it rather charming that Chet chose to play the gallant protector. In a day and age when such efforts might be misconstrued as demeaning to liberated women, the hero role could very well be a dangerous one. And he had a bruise now to prove it. A tinge of guilt made Sky shift in her chair. Certainly, she'd acknowledged handsome men before, but only in a passing, off-handed kind of way. Her reaction to this man, however, stirred a strange and foreign emotion deep inside her.

She'd worked long and hard to earn the scholarships that allowed her to attend Virginia's prestigious School of Veterinary Medicine. Worked even harder to graduate at the top of her class. She'd deliberately filled every hour of every day with work and study and still more work, which left little time for the parties and romance that were so much a part of her classmates' lives. Oh, she'd dated some. Even went steady a time or two. But no male had ever inspired Sky to even consider altering her life's motto. The fact that the handsome cowboy had come to mind dozens of times that day unsettled her.

Leaning back in the comfortable rocker, she pictured Chet—rugged and hard bodied, with hair that caught sunlight like black velvet. A mustachioed, flirty grin. And those smoky gray eyes. "He ain't exactly chicken feed, is he, Face?"

The Irish setter woofed once, as if she understood and agreed.

Sky remembered how her dog came to be called "Face." Face had been sitting on the steps of Sky's Atlanta apartment, staring in that noble Irish setter way. "Just look at that face," Sky had said, crouching and extending a friendly hand to the dog. "C'mere, you big serious looking thing, you." The dog's brows rose; first one, then the other, before she stepped up to sniff Sky's fingertips. "I like that face," Sky said, running both hands alongside the dog's cheeks. Sky found no tags, so she brought the dog inside and cleaned her up.

After feeding the dog a hefty meal, Sky placed an ad in the newspaper and put a few signs on the telephone poles near her building. "We'll give it two weeks," she told the dog. "If nobody claims you by then, you're mine. What do you say to that?" The dog barked once. A quiet, breathy bark that seemed to say, "Okay by me," as the expressive face underlined the idea.

Every day of those two weeks, Sky cringed when the phone rang and each time she picked up the receiver, she hoped and prayed that it wouldn't be the dog's owner. She'd chosen a name but hadn't used it yet, just in case somebody came to claim the beautiful, loving animal. But if the dog stayed with Sky, the Irish setter's name would be Face.

They'd been together three years when Sky made the move back to Montana. The dog had never so much as growled at a living thing, but neither was she overly friendly. Yet she'd walked right up to Chet outside The Grainery, wallowed on the ground at his feet as he ruffled her silky fur, and rewarded his attentions with a lick that left his chin damp. Sky glanced at Face, who lolled contentedly on her back.

"Traitor," she said to her canine companion, smiling and nestling deeper into the oak rocker. Its *squeak, creak, squeak, creak* kept time with cricket chirps.

The phone brought the tranquil moment to a jangling halt. Sky carried her glass of lemonade inside with her. *That's bound to be Dale,* she thought, *probably calling to aim a few more Cupid arrows in my direction.* "Hello," she sang, smiling as she put the receiver to her ear.

"We know you've got those wolf cubs," said the quiet, rasping voice. "Turn 'em loose...or you'll be sorry."

three

The tumbler of lemonade slipped from her hand and crashed to the floor, scattering shards of glass across the black and white tiles. "Who is this!" she demanded.

A quiet click was the answer.

Immediately, she closed and latched the lower half of the dutch door between the kitchen and dining room to keep Face from coming in and cutting her paws on the broken glass. Sky hung up the phone, trying to remember where she'd heard that voice before. "'Turn 'em loose...or you'll be sorry,'" he'd said.

Up there on the plateau, she'd been fairly certain that the gunman had recognized her, thanks to her wild Allen locks. This telephone call was proof that he had. But he'd terrorized her one too many times today. *I refuse to be his willing victim,* she fumed.

"'The Lord is my light and my salvation; whom shall I fear?'" she quoted the twenty-seventh Psalm as she swept up the slivers of glass, remembering the news story she'd read that very afternoon about the hybrid wolf that had killed Bart Laurence's prized bull. The animal had been worth thousands of dollars. Certainly Bart had good reason to fear and hate wolves. But he hadn't been the only one. Joe Wilson's favorite pony had been attacked by a hybrid just last week. Joe had spotted it and fired a shot that scared it off, but not before the half-dog/half-wolf had done enough damage to require Joe to put the pony down. It had been a family pet and its death created quite a stir in Mountain Gate. Pete Miller's had been a horse of a different worth, however. Never one to trust anyone to do what he could do himself, Pete insisted on keeping the thoroughbred, Panache, on his ranch, where he could oversee its feed, exercise, and training between races. Panache had won numerous titles…and plenty of money for Pete. But a hybrid wolf put an end to all that.

Sky filled a bucket with warm sudsy water. As she cleaned up the sticky lemonade spill, she avoided looking at the windows. When she'd scrubbed them during her first week back on Magic Mountain, she'd packed up Gran's frilly white curtains because they interfered with her view of Granite Peak. Now she wished that she'd left them in place, for the black, mirrorlike panes reminded her of two unblinking eyes that watched her every move. If the gunman knew who she was, then he also knew where she lived. Obviously, he meant to exchange the cubs for bounty money, which put Sky smack in the middle, the most dangerous place to be. But she'd made up her mind to protect the cubs, and she wouldn't let them down.

❧

Times, as Gramps had often said, *they were a'changin'.* And Sky knew better than to fight change. So she wasn't surprised when she dumped sixteen window latch sets on the counter at The Grainery first thing the next morning and Martha said, "I thought you Allens didn't believe in locks."

Sky's heart hammered as she recalled the two fuzzy reasons for her purchases. "We do now."

Martha had grown accustomed to hearing people's troubles. When Sky offered no more information, she stuffed the lock kits into a big paper bag. "Chet was in here this morning asking about you," she said, winking.

Sky's brows drew together. "Chet Cozart?"

"One and the same." Martha sighed, then whistled. "Oh

my, but he's a good lookin' fella. If I were twenty years younger...."

The gunshots and the eerie phone call gonged in Sky's memory. Had Chet asked about her out of simple curiosity? Or was he seeking information that would tell him whether or not she harbored the cubs? "What did he want to know?" she asked, her eyes narrowing.

"Oh," Martha began nonchalantly, "he asked how long you'd been away from Mountain Gate, why you'd stayed away so long, whether or not you had a boyfriend...."

Sky's brows rose. "If I had a boyfriend!" Martha had told her yesterday that Chet first came to town with the rodeo. He'd been trampled by a bull, hence, the limp. No doubt, the old woman had given Chet every juicy tidbit about Sky, too. "Okay, so now he knows my entire life's story," Sky said, grinning. "But fair's fair...what about *him*?"

"Chet hasn't had a woman in his life since Ella died." Martha stopped loading the bag. "You knew he married Ella, didn't you?"

Sky nodded. Dale had told her about what the good folks of Mountain Gate had called the romance of the decade.

"Happened a couple of years after your daddy died and you stopped spending summers with your grandparents. He met her in the hospital. After the rodeo accident, don't you know. She was his private duty nurse, see. They'd just celebrated their second anniversary when their little girl was born." Martha peered over her bifocals and shook her head. "It was so sad.... Ella died givin' that child life."

She'd heard Ella had died, but Dale hadn't said how. And Sky hadn't pressed the issue. She hadn't really wanted the details of yet another loss. For ten long years, she'd avoided Mountain Gate because the town, and everyone in it, reminded her of those happy years before her father was killed. Without fail, Dale sent two cards a year, one on her birthday and one at Christmas. But knowing how she felt about Montana memories, the short notes he scribbled in each were simple reminders that they'd be fast friends forever, and nothing more.

"She was healthy right up to the end," Martha was saying. "But the poor little thing just couldn't handle…."

The woman's voice faded into the background as Sky pictured Ella, petite with blue eyes and blond hair. Delicate as porcelain. Sweet as rock candy. It didn't surprise Sky in the least that a function as natural as having a baby had killed her friend. What did surprise Sky was that Ella had married Chet. She'd always insisted she'd never marry a cowboy. Sky wondered what Ella had seen in Chet to make her change her mind.

"How old is their little girl now?" *Their little girl.* It was both pleasant and painful to discover that a tiny piece of her friend lived on in Chet's child.

"Sally? Oh, I'd say she's about five by now. Wait 'til you see her…a miniature Ella. Chet dotes on that kid like she's the last he'll ever have."

Driving back to her ranch, Sky thought about the similarities between Chet's life and her father's. Her heart ached for Chet, forced by circumstances to face parenthood alone. "Treats her like she's the last he'll ever have," Martha had said. *Just like Daddy treated me.*

Sky sighed and turned her attention back to the screwdriver and drill she'd dug out of Wade's big red toolbox. He'd taught her how to use every tool in it. And what he hadn't taught her, Gramps had. As she installed the window locks, Sky tried to picture the gruff, tough cowboy, doting on his tiny daughter. She found it hard to believe he had a gentle bone in his big hard body. Sky thought about him some more as she fed and exercised the cubs…as she pulled a splinter from the paw of Billy Miller's basset hound. In fact, for days now his slanting gray eyes and flirty grin seemed to follow her everywhere she went.

Every time she went into town, Sky looked for his black-windowed gray truck. And, each time it was nowhere to be seen, a note of disappointment rang in her heart. She didn't understand her interest in her dear departed friend's widower. After loving a woman like Ella, Sky couldn't imagine Chet being interested in someone like herself…tall and lanky and still very much a tomboy. *You don't have time for anything but work, anyway*, she reminded herself. *Nothing ventured, nothing lost.*

She knew one way to get the handsome cowboy out of her mind. Sky poured herself a tall glass of lemonade and headed for the front porch. Evenings on the ranch had always been her favorite time of day. Snuggled deep in the red gingham cushions of Gramps' oak rocker, she watched Granite Peak, standing proud and bold against the inky sky. On bright, moonlit nights like this, the ragged mountaintop seemed to glow. She closed her eyes and inhaled crisp clean air.

The cubs had been fed and exercised and the clinic was locked up tight for the night. She'd done the supper dishes and she felt she'd earned these moments of tranquility.

Face's chin rested on her sneakered feet. Crickets chirped. Katydids buzzed. And the old rockers of Gramps' chair creaked softly. She should have felt nothing but peace and contentment. But her brain, swirling with conflicting emotions—fear of the gunman and what other dastardly deeds he might be capable of, pressure of work, her attraction for the tall cowboy—refused to relax. She closed her eyes and forced herself to concentrate on the soothing twilight sounds. Soon, she dozed. It was the first real sleep she'd had in days.

"You're mighty pretty in the moonlight," a voice said.

Jumping with fright, Sky looked toward the voice. Face was already beside him, wagging her tail as she watched him tie his horse to the gate. Sky leaped to her feet. Too quickly, she realized, when dizzying waves shot through her head. In a whipstitch, he was beside her, one big hand supporting her elbow, the other planted firmly against her lower back. He smelled like fresh hay and bath soap.

"Sorry...didn't mean to scare you," he said, his soft breath tickling her ear. "We like to ride after supper," he added, nodding toward his big black mare. "Guess I should have said something sooner, but you looked so peaceful, I didn't want to disturb you."

At first, being in his arms seemed as natural as inhaling and exhaling, but when Sky heard how loudly she was inhaling and exhaling, she stepped back quickly and nearly tumbled down the porch steps. Twice in less than a minute, he saved her from falling. Then, as though he sensed her discomfort at his nearness, Chet pocketed his hands. "Say, that looks tasty...."

She followed his gaze to where her half-filled glass of lemonade sat in a dewy puddle on the table between the chairs. "Would you like some?" A gnawing cold spot pulsed where his hand had touched her back.

"Love some."

She left him and Face on the porch. In the kitchen, picturing the fading bruise she'd caused above his eye, she missed the mouth of his glass and splashed lemonade all over the gleaming white countertop. When she tried to sop it up, she knocked the ice tray to the floor. Sky was on her hands and knees, muttering angrily under her breath, when he joined her in the kitchen.

"One of those days?" he inquired.

A nervous giggle popped from her mouth as she scrambled to her feet. She prided herself on being organized, capable, calm in a storm. So the rapid beating of her heart and the heat in her cheeks puzzled her. She reached for his glass, to hand it to him, just as his fingers closed around it. His skin was rough, yet surprisingly warm. She snatched back her hand and watched him drain, then refill, the glass of lemonade.

"Ahhh." It was a long, satisfied sigh that caused her stomach to flip. "Can't remember when I last had homemade lemonade."

Face woofed, took his shirtsleeve in her teeth, and tugged gently. "Guess she's trying to tell me I've overstayed my welcome," he said, laughing as he stooped to follow the dog onto the porch.

The screen door slammed behind them, the bang reminding Sky of the gunshots that zinged past her on the day she rescued the cubs. When they weren't winking flirtatiously, those glittering, black-lashed orbs could very well be the eyes of a sharpshooter, she realized, more suspicious of his intentions than ever. From the doorway, she said, "What brings you all the way out here?"

Chet had just settled into Gran's black-painted ladder-backed armchair. Shrugging, he flashed a shy half-smile in her direction. "Like I said, Sugar and I always ride after supper." Blinking, he looked at the floor. "Well, that's not entirely true."

His admission quickened her heartbeat.

"It's been a long time since…." Chet paused. "I haven't felt much like…." He cleared his throat and flexed both hands. Then, as though he'd said something he hadn't intended to, he hastily added, "It's been a while since I've met a woman I could have an intelligent conversation with. I thought it might be nice to get better acquainted, since we're practically neighbors, that's all."

Sky sat beside him in Gramps' rocker. Small talk had never been her forte, but she decided she'd better try some on for size if she hoped to find out what, if anything, he knew about her cubs.

Before she could say a word, Chet said, "I met a lady vet in Butte, once." He tipped Gran's ladder-backed chair back on two legs. "Reminded me of old Miss Grundie from the *Archie* comics." He grinned over at her. "I got that picture in my mind every time I heard about a lady doctor after that. Until I met you."

His sideways compliment put a small smile on her face.

"What made you decide to become a veterinarian, anyway?"

She rocked slowly. "Well, when I was six, I found a kitten beside Route 212. Somebody had tossed it from a car, no doubt; it suffered compound fractures of both forelegs. She was coal black with snow white forepaws, so I named her Mittens." Sky took a deep breath, remembering Mittens' pitiful mewing. "She died even before my dad could drive me into town to see the vet. Somehow, I sensed that if I'd known more…known *something* to do right after I found her, Doc Adams might have been able to save her." Looking at him, she ended the story. "When I buried her, I swore I'd never let myself feel that helpless again. I went to the library the very next day and checked out two of James Harriott's books. From that moment on, I was hooked."

Chet smiled and nodded and those warm gray eyes told her that he understood.

Okay, Sky told herself, *forget the gorgeous face and get back to your detective work.* "Martha tells me you're not originally from Montana."

He put all four chair legs back onto the floorboards and rested his glass on his knee. "Born and raised in Wyoming. Fort Washakie, to be exact." Moonlight lit his face, spilled down his chest, and landed in an icy white pool between the pointy toes of his dusty cowboy boots. "After my dad died, my mother and I struck a deal: I'd finish college, and she wouldn't raise a ruckus when I signed on with the rodeo." He put his glass on the table and looked directly at her. "That's how I got this limp, you know."

In response to her silence, he continued. "I was hot to win first prize riding Black Devil—meanest Brahma bull I ever set eyes on. He was pitching and snorting even before we got out of the chute," Chet said. "I should have known he'd be a killer."

Sky wondered if Chet was aware that his big-knuckled hands were gripping the arms of Gran's chair so tightly that his fingertips had turned white.

"I held on for nearly six seconds before he threw me." Shaking his head, Chet added, "Thought he was gonna stomp me into dust. I spent three long weeks at County General, with broken ribs, a punctured lung, my arm in a sling, my leg in traction, and a headache the size of the Grand Canyon. That was the end of my short rodeo career."

She barely knew him, yet the pain in his eyes was as obvious as the mournful coyote song that hung on the breeze. "I'm sorry," she said softly.

"No need to be. If it hadn't been for that accident, I'd never have met Ella." A full minute passed before he added, "She died a while back." He took off his hat and hung it on one knee. "So you knew my Ella?"

Sky swallowed. "Yes. We were best buddies, in fact."

Chet nodded. "Martha told me you spent all your summers here as a kid."

When he looked at her that way, with those *eyes* of his, Sky held her breath. She hadn't known what to expect when she'd started her mini-investigation, but opening old wounds hadn't been on the list. He said "my Ella," not with the voice of a man who believed his wife to be property, but with the soft sweet tones of innocent, lasting love.

"She left me the prettiest little daughter a man could hope to have."

According to Martha, Ella had died five years ago, but the slight catch in his voice made it apparent to Sky that for Chet, the pain was still very much part of his life. The tenderness in his eyes and voice when he spoke of her friend only made Sky like him more.

Suddenly, he sat up and leaned his elbows on his knees. "Well, enough about me. Tell me, what are you doing way out here all by yourself? You'd make a lot more money in a big city."

"True," Sky nodded, "but I wouldn't have that view."

Together, they gazed toward Granite Peak, cloaked by the deep purple night sky. The hazy, mystical view was responsible for the name her soft-hearted, poetic grandfather had given the property: Magic Mountain.

"You've got a point there," Chet said, his voice a near whisper.

Spending so much time with animals had honed Sky's ability to analyze demeanor and attitude. She sensed that Chet was a good and decent man. A man who could be trusted with any secret, even one as dark and dangerous as hers. She wondered what he'd say if he knew she was raising two wolf cubs, what he'd do if he found out that she intended to continue to work with them until they were old enough to survive on their own in the wild.

Quickly, she came to her senses. His whole life was

livestock, in one way or another. Martha told her that Chet now owned Four Aces. Maybe it had been at his command that Bud posted the steadily rising wolf bounty in the first place. *Just stick to the plan,* she warned herself, *and keep your mouth shut about those cubs!*

Several moments ticked by as they gazed at the night sky, content, it seemed, to enjoy the awesome beauty and silence that surrounded them. Sky's wristwatch beeped, cracking the stillness and startling them both. Their eyes locked, and they burst into a tension-reducing round of laughter.

Face woofed.

"My sentiments exactly." He patted the dog's head, then stood. "Guess I'd better head on out."

She didn't believe it had been him shooting at her that day. In fact, something inside her made Sky want to share her secret more than ever. In that moment of weakness, she nearly admitted how much she'd enjoyed his visit. Almost asked him, to quote May West, "Come back and see me, any old time." But before her tongue could form the words, old ghosts reared their ugly heads. *Nothing ventured, nothing lost*, Sky reminded herself.

"Thanks for the drink…and the company."

Her life's motto clear in her mind, Sky realized she'd better keep a safe distance from this man if she hoped to live by it. In a deliberately steely voice, she said, "You're quite welcome."

He tore his gaze from the glowing horizon to meet her dark eyes. The furrowed brow and tight-lipped pout, visible in the shaft of moonlight that slanted across his handsome features, told Sky that her cool response had stung like a slap. *Well,* she asked herself, *what did he expect…a big juicy good night kiss!*

As if he had heard her thoughts, Chet licked his lips. "Guess

I'll be on my way, then." His boots thumped down the wooden porch steps and over the flagstone walk.

Though he tried hard to hide it, the effects of his run-in with the Brahma were obvious. Sky wondered if he limped because it hurt to walk, or simply because the bull's hooves had permanently damaged muscle and bone. She preferred the latter; having lost the love of his life, he'd already suffered enough pain. If Sky didn't know anything else, she knew how much it hurt to lose someone you loved.

From the other side of the fence, he climbed into the saddle and saluted. "G'night," he said, and sent her the cowboy salute by touching a finger to the brim of his hat. "Maybe I'll see you in town sometime." With that, he rode away.

Face jumped up and rested her front paws between the fence's picket points and watched until he disappeared from sight. She cast a backward glance in the direction of her mistress and whined.

"Oh, don't give me that," Sky scolded half-heartedly. "It isn't *my* fault your pal left."

In response, Face barked once, trotted past Sky and onto the porch, where she flopped in a graceless heap. Her actions made it very clear who, in her opinion, had been responsible for the departure of her new friend.

⋰

Deep in the night, Sky was dreaming of Chet's handsome half-grin when the ringing phone woke her. "Hello?" The clock on the nightstand said 3:47.

When no one responded, Sky sat up, wide awake and remembering the terrifying call she'd received on the day she found the cubs. "Hello?" she repeated, hoping this wasn't a repeat performance.

"Do yourself a big favor, Doc. Turn those critters loose, right now, and nobody will get hurt."

"Who *is* this!" she demanded. Since there had been just the one call in the days that had followed the cubs' rescue, she'd allowed herself to slip into a comfortable, confident routine. She'd chalked up the first threat as a mistake, and told herself the caller had seen the error of his ways. Maybe he'd already paid a little visit to Magic Mountain and, after a quick investigation, satisfied himself that no wolf cubs lived there.

The dial tone droned in her ear. Replacing the receiver in its cradle, she considered calling someone for help. But she realized no one could help her.

She wished she could talk to the marksman. Tell him she understood his hatred of hybrid wolves. Fear of man had been bred out of the half-dog/half-wolves, and they now sometimes attacked livestock. The ranchers, after getting no help or support from the government, adopted a credo, "The only good wolf is a dead wolf."

Sky knew her cubs' mother had been a hybrid, and may very well have cost some rancher a prized bull or a favorite horse. But the vigilante mentality had turned ugly. And now, purebred wolves, whose numbers were already reduced, were on the hit list, too, though their fear of man remained firmly entrenched and they rarely wandered into human territory. But none of that mattered now. What did matter was that the cubs were as defenseless as the ranchers' livestock. Sky wanted to give the wolves a fighting chance at survival, nothing more.

Roaming from window to window through her darkened house, Face close at her heels, Sky peered into the shadowy yard, wondering if the caller and the shooter were one and the same person, or if his plural references really meant he belonged to a group of bounty hunters. A creepy crawly, somebody's-out-there feeling prickled on the back of her neck, and she had the distinct impression she was being watched. Hugging herself, Sky prowled the house all night, stopping only now and then to sit stiff-backed in a chair or lie rigid on her bed, wide awake, listening, aware....

At first light, she grabbed her dad's police binoculars and positioned herself in the middle of the yard. Rotating slowly, she examined the horizon. Finding no evidence that anyone had set up a lookout somewhere beyond Magic Mountain's property lines, she headed for the shelter to feed and exercise the cubs in the tiny, fenced space behind the house.

Gran used to say, "Idle hands are the devil's workshop." Sky supposed the old saying could just as easily apply to worry. Long hours and hard work had helped her survive Wade's violent death; the same medicine would see her through this ordeal, she reasoned. So she got up a little earlier every day, worked a little longer and harder with the cubs, and extended the clinic hours so she could tend to a few more patients. A weed wouldn't dare show its head in the garden, and dust was afraid to settle in the house. Sky fell into bed exhausted each night...praying the phone wouldn't ring. Each morning when she woke, her first thoughts were of the cubs.

Because she'd found them where a gnarled pine grew from a boulder, Sky named the female Piney and the male Rocky. Daily, she scribbled wolf-related statistics under column headings she'd printed on the left side of the ledger style book: Exercise. Play. Instinctual Behavior. Learned Behavior. Weight. Meals. On the right-hand pages, Sky charted more specific observations such as, "It took three weeks to coax them to go up and down the shelter stairs."

Her med-school work with the Alaskan wolves had taught her most of what she needed to know about the species. The shelter, as it turned out, was the perfect home for them, for it protected the cubs not only from being seen, but from seeing things they should avoid once she returned them to the wild. Cars, airplanes, lawn mowers, and other machines of man would still terrify them long after they'd been released in the foothills. Most important of all, the sight, scent, and sound of humans—other than herself—would send them high-tailing it for cover. And because domestic animals also carried faint human scents, the cubs would be equally wary of live-stock and pets...with the exception of Face, of course.

"For the past two days," she wrote in the journal, "Rocky and Piney have responded to hand clapping by running to me." She clapped and waited for the customary *clickety-clack* of their toenails as they scrambled down the narrow wooden staircase that led into the cool cavernous shelter. Giving each cub a hearty "hello" hug, Sky laughingly endured their damp smooches.

"You guys have bad breath," she said, ruffling their soft, silvery fur. "Haven't you ever heard of a little invention called the toothbrush?"

The Irish setter, wiggling herself into the fuzzy circle, licked Sky's cheek, then slobbered on each cub.

"They sure grow on you, don't they, girl?"

Face answered with a happy bark and a doggy smile. The cubs growled and rolled playfully on the cool concrete floor as Sky laughed at their noisy, affectionate display of cousinly love.

"Are you lookin' to get shot?" thundered an angry male voice.

four

He looked like he owned the place, leaning casually against the door frame, dark brows drawn together above those gun-metal gray eyes.

His presence thrilled yet intimidated Sky. "What are *you* doing here?"

"Now, what kind of a greeting is that?"

His voice, so smug and self-assured, grated in her ears. "The only kind you'll get when you sneak around and scare people half to death."

"Well, at least you have the good sense to *be* scared," he thundered. "Are you ready to load up those critters and put 'em back where they belong before somebody gets 'hurt?" he asked, nodding toward the cubs.

Ignoring his question, she posed one of her own. "Exactly who do you think you are, coming over here uninvited, barking orders like some Marine drill sergeant?"

He stood there, shifting a toothpick from one side of his mouth to the other, as if willing her to realize how silly it was to think she could actually prepare the cubs for release in the foothills.

If I had an ounce more courage, she thought, *I'd march over there and slap that insolent smirk off his face.* Instead, she asked, "What do you want?"

He removed the toothpick from between his lips, inspected it for a long, silent moment, then returned it to the far left corner of his mustachioed mouth and crossed one booted foot in front of the other. "Let's just say I'm a very curious fel-

low." The toothpick traveled again. "I saw fur on your shirt
the other night in your kitchen, and it's been bugging me ever
since."

Sky pointed at Face, who sat beside him, looking up into
his face like a devoted cult follower. "And I'm a veterinarian."

He shook his head and grinned. "That you are. But Face,
here, is a redhead, like you. The fur I saw was gray...coarse."
The grin disappeared when he said, "Like wolf fur." He stared
at her for a full minute before adding, "Yesterday, I overheard a couple of my cowhands talking about a she-wolf
they'd shot two, three weeks ago; said Bart Laurence gave
'em a grand for her carcass." He squatted in the doorway to
drape an arm around Face. "They've been looking for her
cubs ever since."

He met her eyes with such intensity it caused Sky to swal-
low, hard.

"Too much of a coincidence, or could that have been the
same wolf?" he asked, his voice surprisingly gentle, despite
the steely glow from his eyes. "If anybody was going to rescue a couple of orphaned wolf cubs, it'd be you."

The cubs sat side by side, staring at Chet. Oddly, they
didn't seem the least bit afraid of him. Quite the contrary,
she noted as their dog lips pulled back in matching canine
grins. Sky adjusted the glow of the battery powered lantern
on the table near the door.

"Let's take this discussion outside," she said. "I don't want
you upsetting them." She snapped her fingers. "Upstairs,
Face." The dog immediately dashed up the steps, followed
closely by Chet, while Sky stayed behind to bolt the thick
metal door.

"Unreasonable, ridiculous," he muttered as he walked past
her, flapping his arms like a giant bird, "afraid to talk in front

of animals!" In the shed, he folded his arms over his chest, planted his feet a shoulder's width apart, and watched her drop the trap door into place. Outside, as she snapped the padlock shut, he assumed the same stance.

Pocketing the key, Sky said, "This way, Mr. Clean," and led the way into the kitchen, where she filled two mugs with hot coffee. In half an hour, the sun would be up, but now, the house was still early morning bleak. Sky turned on the overhead light. "Milk and sugar?"

"Just black, thanks." Chet put his hat on the table, then turned a kitchen chair around and sat down, his big arms resting on the back of the chair.

Sky sat across from him at the table.

"How could anyone so smart do anything so foolish?" he demanded. "Don't you know there's a bounty on their heads?"

"It's precisely *because* of the bounty that I'm doing this! I was there when their mother was killed. I couldn't very well let them be shot, too."

Chet sighed. "Under similar circumstances, I'd probably have done the same thing," he admitted, his dark brows knitted with worry. "But letting them die might have been the most humane thing you could have done in the long run—for everybody concerned."

Exasperated, she blew a stream of air through her lips.

"Look," he said, folding his huge hands on the table top, "I know it's your business to protect and care for animals. But this situation is different than most. Be realistic, why don't you? If certain people find out what you're doing, you could be in as much danger as those pups out there."

She met his eyes, and it surprised her to find such honest concern there. Still, something made her say, "Certain people? People like *you,* maybe?"

He let the question pass, unanswered.

"I won't let them die for a few measly dollars."

"When a smart person sees danger, he hides from it but a simple person just goes on and suffers because of it."

She'd incorrectly made the assumption that Chet was not a follower. But the quick, easy way he'd paraphrased Proverbs told her otherwise…and she added that fact to her "Reasons to Like the Cowboy" list.

"Let me ask you a question," she said, drumming her fingers on the table. "Dale seems to think you're a pretty decent guy. Why'd you post that bounty in the first place?"

Chet's brows rose so quickly, Sky was afraid they'd collide with his hairline. "I didn't. Bart Laurence did. And Bud followed suit."

"Well, it's *your* ranch. I'd think—"

"Look," he began, his eyes darkening and his voice dangerously low, "you don't know much about me and my ranch. I suggest you stick to discussing subjects you *do* know something about."

His flinty-eyed scrutiny unnerved her, but to keep him from seeing it, Sky took a long drink of her coffee.

He ran both hands through his hair and held them there a moment, then took a deep breath, as if trying to decide whether to bother telling Sky how he came to own Four Aces.

She watched his forefinger slide back and forth on the black felt of his hat, raising and flattening the velvety material. Sky thought he looked incredibly handsome, lost in thought like that.

When he met her eyes again, he said, "Here's the way it was: The Houghtons and the Laurences have been battling over the boundary between Four Aces and the Lazy L for generations. One night Bud and Bart, Senior got involved in a poker game, and the two old fools bet land instead of money. Bud lost. And the acreage he lost just so happened to have on it the only water supply for miles. He'd have gone under for sure without that parcel.

"So I waited until Bart, Senior sobered up. I couldn't just stand there like a fence post and watch Ella suffer a lifetime for one night of her father's drunken stupidity. I made Bart an offer he couldn't refuse: Half a million if he'd forget the bet. The deal was, he'd keep his big yap shut about my part in it. But they got tanked up again a couple months later, and Bart spilled the beans.

"Bud had been losing money every year for a decade. I have a Master's degree in economics. I promised him I'd get the place humming again. That way, he had Ella and the ranch to boot."

"And did you save the ranch?" Sky asked.

The well-arched left brow rose and he grinned openly. "Turned a profit that first year and, despite this rotten economy, we've been holding our own ever since."

"So now the ranch is yours...."

Chet grimaced. "There you go again, talking about things you know nothing about." He sipped his coffee. "When Ella died, Bud lost all interest in the place. Said he'd rather see me at the helm than watch the place go to pot. So, yes. It's mine...on paper. But it's really Bud's. Always will be."

"Very big of you to let him stay at Four Aces all these years."

Chet's brows rose high on his forehead. He laughed. "You don't know me well enough to have such a low opinion of me, Doc." The smile in his eyes dimmed when he added, "What kind of man would I be if I kicked the old coot out, just because I *could*?"

Sky didn't have a low opinion of him, at all. In fact, she admired and respected him for what he'd done. That she thought so highly of Chet so soon after meeting him frightened her. Stubbornly, she clung tighter to her life's motto. "What does any of that have to do with allowing Bud to post a bounty?"

His stare hardened. "First of all, nobody *allows* Bud Houghton to do anything. And second, I'm half Cheyenne. I probably know as much about wolves as...as even a *veterinarian*."

She ignored his sarcastic tone.

"They're beautiful intelligent beasts. And most of the time," he continued, his face and attitude gentling, "I wish we still lived back in the days when survival of the fittest was the law of the land. I'd never stoop so low as to pay to have even one wolf killed."

Quickly, he added, "Which isn't to say I wouldn't shoot a wolf myself if I caught one trying to make a meal of one of my cows. You'll find I'm someone who'll do whatever it takes to protect what's mine."

Finally, she saw the position he was in. As a rancher, Chet was duty bound to protect the livestock that were the financial support of his family and employees, but as a man, he respected wolves.

Handsome. Intelligent. Honest. Big-hearted to a fault. Sky liked him too much. But she felt obliged, because of her life's motto, to stifle the feelings before they got out of hand. "Nothing justifies killing innocent—"

"Innocent!" he interrupted. "When those critters are older, they'll kill their share of cattle in a season. That's hardly my idea of innocent."

"But they kill by instinct and only then to survive," she said.

"That's all the ranchers are trying to do," he answered.

His quiet logic unnerved her. Sky's grandparents had spent a lifetime striving to eke by on rancher's meager wages. She knew exactly how hard life out here could be. But that didn't change one thing in her mind. "Survival of the fittest," she said.

Chet could only shake his head.

"I need to know what your intentions are," Sky said.

His gorgeous gray eyes widened. "My intentions?"

Sky believed the cubs deserved to live as nature meant them to. If when she released them, they didn't survive Mother Nature or the bounty hunters, so be it, but she intended to at least give them a fighting chance. "I can't let you tell anyone about them." She hoped the desperation in her heart wasn't evident in her voice.

One corner of his mouth lifted in wry amusement. "You can't *let* me? And exactly how do you plan to stop me?"

Sky lowered her eyes and listened to her hammering heart. There had to be a way to convince him to keep her secret. If he didn't, she'd be powerless to save the cubs, and she knew it. Worse, still, she knew that Chet knew it, too. She gulped her coffee and took her time swallowing it. Whether it was his penetrating gaze or the titillating grin or the big-hearted nature that inspired his actions toward Bud, she didn't know, but something inside her made Sky trust him.

"I only want to keep them safe until they're old enough to fend for themselves. Give me three months," she added, no longer caring whether or not he heard the pleading note in her voice. "Three months, and I'll release them in the foothills. I promise."

Face padded into the kitchen and sat beside Chet. "She wants to keep them safe until they're old enough to fend for themselves," he told the dog. "I say she's plumb loco. What do you think?"

The dog barked once and put her paw on Chet's thigh.

Patting Face's head, Chet looked deep into Sky's eyes.

"You're either as dumb as they come," he said, left brow rising slowly, "or the bravest woman I've ever met."

Shifting uncomfortably in her seat, Sky didn't know whether he'd just paid her a compliment or slapped her with an insult. "Does that mean you won't tell anyone? You'll keep my secret?"

Chet's thumb and forefinger smoothed his mustache. "Hmmm. It might be interesting to watch you teach them how to behave like proper wolves."

Feeling simultaneously safe and elated, Sky impulsively covered his hands with her own. "Thank you, Chet. Thank you."

He looked at their mound of fingers. After a long moment, he met her eyes. "Don't thank me just yet, Doc," he said, his voice soft and somber. "I may very well have just signed their death warrants…and yours, too."

Readjusting their hands so that his blanketed hers, he added, "You're going to have to be very careful from here on out. I'm not the only one who can add two and two."

"Two and two?"

"A veterinarian," he said, holding his forefinger up between their faces. His middle finger joined the first when he added, "and wolf cubs on the loose. You're not exactly well positioned, out here in the middle of nowhere, y'know." Chet seemed aware that his statement frightened her, for he released his eye lock on her and focused for a moment on their hands, still entwined on the table. When he met her eyes again, he said, "Yeah, I'll keep your little secret…on one condition."

It took a moment for it to sink in. First he'd scared her half to death by listing the reasons she was a potential target. And then, with no warning whatever, he did a complete turnabout and added a condition to the deal. Sky snatched back her hands, fear replaced by fury. "I might have known you'd be the type to issue ultimatums!" Leaning forward, she said through clenched teeth, "All right, Mr. Cozart. Go ahead. Name your condition."

The barest hint of a smile glimmered in his eyes, and he said with deliberate slowness: "Dinner."

Sky blinked. She'd expected him to ask for free veterinary services. Maid service, maybe. But dinner?

As if he read her mind, he repeated, "Dinner."

Chet stood and branded her with his smoky gaze. He hadn't been able to do a single thing to protect Ella, but he decided he'd make Sky see that trying to raise those cubs could be deadly, even if it took the whole night. Then, maybe, if he was lucky, by the time the dessert cart rolled around, he'd have convinced her to turn the beasts loose.

Her dark eyes narrowed. "I don't get it."

"You don't have to get it," he said. "You just have to be ready at seven. We're going to Livingston."

Livingston was an hour's drive north of Mountain Gate. Mentally, she calculated the evening: An hour to get there, another for the meal, one to get home…. Sky didn't know if she could stand to be alone with him that long. But her cubs' lives depended on his silence.

He thrust out his right hand. "Deal?"

Hesitantly, she put hers into it. "Deal."

Chet squeezed, ever so gently, looked deep into her eyes, and released her. Without another word, he grabbed his hat and headed for the back door. Then, as if he'd overlooked something important, he stopped, one hand on the doorknob, and faced her.

Here it comes, she told herself, *the real condition.*

"This restaurant I have in mind," he said, "is pretty classy. In case you're wondering how to dress, I mean …." As quickly as he'd said it, he was gone, black hat and all.

Face stared at the closed door and whimpered.

"Yeah, I know," Sky said. "There he goes again, riding off into the sunset." She noticed the bright fireball, rising slowly in the morning sky. "I stand corrected: Into the sun*rise*."

ॐ

All day long, Sky found herself wishing she had more to keep her mind occupied, so she could concentrate on work, rather than the evening ahead. Unfortunately, it had been a slow day at the clinic. She spent several hours in the gardens, pulling up the last of the exhausted flower and vegetable plants she'd put in during her first days in Mountain Gate. But no matter how hard she tried, her thoughts returned to their morning conversation. A grating voice in her head whispered, *He could be the shooter,* while a gentle, sweet voice in her heart sighed, *You can trust him.* Sky wanted to trust him, but she'd spent so many years living by her motto, she wondered if she remembered how.

five

Sky barely recognized Chet when he arrived, wearing a navy blue suit and a starched white shirt. His maroon tie was in such sharp contrast to his eyes that they looked more rainy-day gray than ever.

"Well, look at you," he said, walking one big circle around her. "I must admit, you clean up real good."

She grinned at his sideways compliment. The peach chiffon had always been Sky's favorite dress. She spent most of her life wearing jeans and tee shirts under her lab coats—hardly feminine attire. In this dress, she felt feminine, lady-like, even pretty.

"Do we have reservations?" she asked as he helped her into her coat.

"Don't need 'em," he said. "I have connections at this particular establishment." With that, he bowed low and opened the door. "Your chariot awaits, m'lady."

In place of the ominous looking dark-windowed truck he usually drove, a silver Porsche convertible sat in her driveway. "Christmas present to myself last year," he explained as she locked her front door, "when I decided it was time to start living my life again. Hope you don't mind the inconvenience of a low rider."

Ella flitted through Sky's mind at his mention of living again. But his happy attitude was contagious, and she grinned, too. Sky hadn't expected to enjoy the evening, but already, she was grinning.

"I hope you don't plan to put the top down."

"Maybe on the drive home," he said, winking as he opened the car door, "when it won't matter if you get...mussed."

She slid onto the leather passenger seat, carefully avoiding his eyes. The tone of his deep voice alone had been more than suggestive enough; if she'd found the same expression in his eyes, Sky no doubt would have a blush to hide.

He'd chosen a classical string concerto to entertain them on the car's CD player as they drove and, from time to time, he drew her attention to sights that hadn't been part of Montana's scenery during the time when she'd spent every summer on Magic Mountain.

His connections at the restaurant, as it turned out, were the owners.

"Thees place, she ees all mine, thanks to Meester Chet," Pablo explained after Chet introduced him to Sky. "You see, thee bank refuse to lend us thee money." He winked at Chet. "But Meester Chet, he know I can cook, and that my Maria, she can bake fine cakes and breads. Weethout thee loan from heem, Maria, she would still be thee cook at Four Aces, and me, I would still be thee gardener."

Sky had never seen a man blush before. But there Chet stood, all six-feet-three-inches of him, pink-cheeked as a boy on his first date. He tried to shush Pablo, but the shorter man ignored him, took Sky's arm and led her to a table in a quiet corner of the restaurant.

"Meester Cozart, he would not even charge us eenterest. Thees is one fine man, for sure. You some lucky young lady for to be hees companion, yes?"

Smiling, Sky glanced at Chet, whose tanned cheeks still glowed. That he'd tried to keep his wonderful deed a secret only made him more appealing. "Yes," she admitted, "I suppose I am a lucky young lady at that."

"I leave you now," Pablo said, "but I return *un minuto* with a menu. No charge," he added, and when Chet opened his mouth to protest, Pablo stamped one foot and wagged his finger in the air. "Thees ees my place, no? I am thee boss, and what I say, she is law!"

During dinner, as Chet entertained her with stories about his life as a rodeo star, Sky found it increasingly difficult to stick to her plan. Pablo's story made it impossible to continue thinking of Chet as a hard-hearted, wolf-hating rancher. And when he pulled out his wallet to show off photos of his little girl, the warmth in his voice and the pride in his eyes made Sky recall her relationship with her own father. Her dad had taught her how foolhardy it could be to judge people by first impressions. Sky understood better than ever why, because if she had allowed herself to form an opinion of Chet based on their first encounter, she'd never have discovered what a warm, witty, wonderful man he truly was.

In the ladies' room after dinner, as she combed her hair, Sky couldn't help thinking what a lucky little girl Sally was to have a father like Chet. Sky had grown up surrounded by that same huge kind of love until just days before her seventeenth birthday when a bank robber killed Wade, her father. Wade had been so much more than just her dad. He'd been advisor, protector, and, most of all, her friend. Ten years had passed, yet the ache of missing him was as big as ever.

"Is something the matter, honey?" the woman at the next sink asked. "Looks like you've seen a ghost."

Sky smiled stiffly, and trembled as she stuffed her lipstick back into her purse. "I'm fine, thanks." Her emotions were dangerously close to the surface, and Sky squared her shoulders, determined as always, to keep the memories in their proper place.

He watched her cross the blue-carpeted floor, and the closer she got to their table, the wider his grin grew. "I thought maybe

you'd fallen in," he said, standing as she took her seat. "I was
about to dial nine-one-one."

Her father had that same gift for turning cloudy moments
into sunny ones. "Why cry over spilt milk," Wade would say,
"when it's so much more fun to lap it up!" She wanted to
forget her moment of weakness in the ladies' room, she wanted
to concentrate on being with Chet. And it wasn't difficult.
He'd made a great effort to see to it that she enjoyed the
evening. Why, he hadn't mentioned the cubs even once!

As they exchanged philosophical and political opinions, she
discovered they had many things in common. They'd voted
for the same man in the last election. Both became outraged
at the mention of flag burning. And each loved kids and dogs
and apple pie.

Sky remembered the night he'd dropped by her house, saying it had been a long time since he'd had an intelligent conversation with a woman. She was wondering what sorts of
women he'd been seeing since Ella's death when the lady
from the restroom walked by, reminding Sky where her mind
had been only moments ago. She took a deep breath and said
a quick prayer that her melancholy mood would soon pass.
She owed him that much, at least, for not subjecting her to a
cub safety lecture.

"Dessert?" the waiter asked, rolling the dessert cart up to
their table. Sky smiled as Chet rubbed his palms together.

"I'll take a slice of the lemon meringue pie," he said, grinning. "Sky, what'll you have?"

He'd never said her name before. It sounded lyrical and
poetic, coming from his lips. "I'm not very hungry," she admitted. "Maybe I'll just have a bite of yours?"

His flirty grin made her stomach flip and her heart lurch.
Then Chet turned to the waiter and held up one finger, then
two. "One pie, two forks." And when the tuxedoed young

man moved on to the next table, Chet placed his hand on top of hers. "You're so quiet all of a sudden. You feeling okay?"

She took a sip of water. "The way you were talking about Sally reminded me of my dad. We were close, the way you two are. It reminded me of how much I miss him. But I'm fine. Really."

"Martha told me he was a cop. A sheriff, I believe she said." His brow furrowed. "Died in the line of duty?"

Sky nodded. "Took a bullet intended for a bank teller." The telling of it sounded so cold and mechanical that she quickly added, "He died in my arms. I felt so completely helpless, watching the life go right out of him." Two tellers and one bank patron had witnessed the grisly scene. Those facts had gone into the police report, of course, but she'd never told another living soul about the moment Wade died. Sky grabbed the water goblet again and hoped it would hide her trembling lips.

Chet's gentle grip on her free hand tightened, and his gray eyes said what his words needn't have: "I'm sorry, Sky."

Shrugging, she sat up straighter and put the glass at the high noon spot above her plate. She drew a *W* in the condensation on its bowl. "There isn't a person alive who doesn't have a sad story to tell. You know that as well as I do."

He withdrew his hand and, for a moment, busied himself by adjusting his tie, examining his fingernails, straightening his jacket. Then he smiled. "Not one to beat around the bush, are you?" Sky was beginning to like the way his left brow lifted when he asked a question. In fact, she was beginning to like a lot of things about him. She realized that if she hoped to continue living by her life's motto, she'd have to exercise a lot of caution when dealing with this charming man.

When the waiter returned and put the dessert plate in front

of him, Chet accepted only one fork. Carefully, he cut off the point of the pie and held it in front of Sky's face. "You first."

She'd seen this in the movies, and hesitated, afraid she might open her mouth too wide, or not wide enough, and pie would end up on her face, or worse, in her lap. But Chet skillfully slid the bite into her mouth, his lips parting slightly as he watched hers open to accept his offering.

"Thwnkym," she said around it.

He'd already popped a sizeable chunk into his own mouth. "Ywr wrlcm."

They seemed to share one thought: All dressed up like respectable adults, but talking with their mouths full, like a couple of unruly kids. Their laughter brought inquisitive stares from nearby diners.

"I do believe," he said between snickers, "we're making public spectacles of ourselves."

He chose that exact relaxed moment to reach out and remove a tiny crumb of pie crust from her lower lip. The pressure of his thumb, lingering there, seemed natural and normal. Their eyes fused on a familiar sizzling current, reminding Sky of the day they'd met, when she'd vowed to win their staring match. Though she broke the visual connection, Sky sensed that she and Chet were still attached mentally. She began looking for things to dislike, to make living by her life's motto easier. But try as she might, Sky couldn't find a single thing wrong with Chet. In fact, she felt as though she'd known him for years.

"I can't believe my big mouth tonight," he said as they crossed the darkened parking lot to his car. "I don't think I've talked this much, all at one time, ever before in my life." He slipped an arm around her waist. "I hope you won't think I'm a complete boor for dominating the conversation all evening."

Teasing and flirting had never been part of Sky's personality. Yet with Chet, the two went hand-in-hand as naturally as the stars went with the inky sky above. "Well, not a *complete* boor, anyway," she said, looking up at him.

&

The pleasant chatter they'd enjoyed in the restaurant continued all during the hour's drive home. He'd chosen a collection of old country and western classics and, from time to time, sang a line or two along with Willie or Patsy. Sky enjoyed every note, even though his singing reminded her more of a rusty hinge than any melody she'd ever heard.

When he parked the Porsche in front of her house, he turned in the seat and placed a big, warm hand on her shoulder. "How about a cup of coffee?"

Sky's heart fluttered. She could barely make out his features in the darkness, yet somehow she knew those crisp gray eyes were boring into her, hoping for an affirmative answer. As she'd dressed for dinner, she'd planned to be gracious and polite and nothing more, no matter what he said, for the cubs' sake. But he hadn't mentioned them once. She'd appreciated that. "High test or decaf?"

As they walked slowly up her flagstone walk, he draped an arm across her shoulders. Sky liked the warm weight of it and resisted the urge to lace her fingers in his.

While she prepared the pot, he sat where he had that very morning. "So, tell me, are you a good cook?" His big thumb wiped pepper powder from the top of the shaker on the table.

"I'm no gourmet," she said, putting two cups and saucers on the table, "but I can whip up a respectable meat and potatoes meal."

He nodded approvingly. "Most professional women I've known aren't very comfortable in the kitchen."

She wondered what it was about him that brought out this

outrageously flirtatious side of her personality. Grinning, she said, "There's not a gadget in this room that scares me, mister."

Suddenly, the friendly light in his eyes dimmed. "Yeah. You're just all kinds of brave, aren't you?"

Here comes the speech, she warned herself.

In response to her stiff-backed silence, Chet held up his hands in mock surrender. "Hey, far be it from me to tell you how to live your life...however little there may be left to live."

"I appreciate your concern, Chet. But I've been on my own for a long time. I know how to take care of myself."

He rubbed the spot above his eye, where she'd hit him on the day they met. "So you said."

At least his mischievous grin was back. Sky hadn't realized how much she'd enjoyed looking at it until it disappeared. Finally, the pot hissed, its signal that the coffee was ready. "You take yours black, right?"

Face sat beside him, panting for a pat on the head. "Brave as a lion, with a memory like an elephant. She's in the right line of work, wouldn't you say?" he asked the dog, whose teeth clicked in a happy, breathy bark.

Chet took his time drinking the coffee, then helped himself to a second cup, warming hers when he did. For the next twenty minutes, he talked nonstop about the various consequences of trying to raise two hybrid wolf cubs. Finally, lectured out and his cup empty, he stood. "Promise me something," he said, holding her hand as they crossed the wood-floor foyer. "Promise you'll be careful when you go to the shelter. You never know who might be watching."

"I'll be careful," she said, her voice a bored monotone.

Both hands on her shoulders, he stopped her. "I'm serious, Sky. You're totally unprotected out here. Somebody with binoculars could watch from any direction, and you'd never know it."

Narrowing her eyes, she regarded him with sudden suspicion. She thought she saw him blush, but he moved toward the door so quickly, she couldn't be sure.

"For your information," he volunteered, "I was looking for a lost foal the other day. I was miles away, yet I saw you go into that shed and you didn't come out for hours." His eyes darkened and his brows drew together. "You're just lucky I'm not one of the bounty hunters."

Sky frowned. "Oh, why don't you just call off the stupid bounty?"

"I didn't post it, remember? Besides, it's too late for that. There're enough side bets to make up for any bounty Bud or Bart could afford to pay."

"Side bets?"

He took a deep breath and stared at the ceiling for a moment. When he met her eyes again, Chet said, "The guys are betting a month's pay…whoever bags the cubs first gets everybody else's salary."

She sighed. "You make it sound as if we're at war."

"Haven't you been reading the papers?"

She remembered the wolf war headlines. "Intelligent people don't pay any attention to that kind of news."

"Intelligent people don't harbor thousands of dollars' worth of wolf on their property and risk being drummed out of business…or killed."

She was about to respond to his "intelligent people" comment when the rest of his statement caught her attention. "Do you really think it's that serious?"

"You bet I do."

Sky wanted to wish the whole mess away. But she'd always been a woman of her word. For better or worse, she was all the protection the cubs had. "If I let them go now, they'll die for sure. Even if the bounty hunters didn't get them, the coyotes would. Or they'd starve to death. And they'd never be accepted by a pack, because they don't know the first thing about—"

With no warning, he gathered her in a warm, protective embrace. Automatically, her arms went around him.

"What am I gonna do with you?" he sighed into her hair. "You're as big-hearted and pigheaded as they come," he added, kissing the top of her head, "and while that's a mighty delicious combination, I have a ranch to run and a daughter to raise. I can't be running over here morning and night to stand guard while you tend those critters."

She broke free of his hold and stood, her hands forming fists at her sides. "So who asked you to! I can take—"

"Care of myself," he finished, rolling his eyes. "I know, I know." It was his turn to sound bored. Chet opened the door slightly, then clicked it shut it again. "I never meant to insult you, Sky. I hope you know that. It's just that I'm worried about what could happen to you, all alone, all the way out here in the middle of nowhere. I can't seem to make you understand that you could be in real danger."

No one had cared what happened to her…not since Wade. Sky was touched by his genuine concern. "I understand. And I'll be fine."

Chet grabbed her wrist and pulled her to him. "You're a stubborn, infuriating woman, Sky Allen," he rasped, his lips fractions of an inch from hers.

In the dim light of the foyer lamp, his eyes glittered like hard gray diamonds as they flicked from her mouth to her throat to her eyes. She wondered what that thick, dark mustache might feel like against her lips, and she held her breath as she waited for his kiss. He inhaled deeply and stepped back. "You'd better be careful. That's all I can say. Because if anything happens to you…."

If anything happens to me…you'll what? she wondered. And during the pause, Sky thought maybe he'd changed his mind; maybe he wanted that kiss after all.

Instead, he cupped her chin in his palm. Shaking his head, he repeated, "I mean it. Be careful!"

As his Porsche roared off, Sky touched the spot where his fingers had warmed her skin, still wondering how his lips might have felt against hers.

&

After Sky had fed and exercised Rocky and Piney and secured them in the shelter, she made night rounds in the clinic. She'd neutered Spuds, a fat Siamese cat, that morning and he glowered at her as she inspected his incision. "You're healing up nicely, fella," she said, smoothing his soft, multicolored coat. "And don't look at me like that; you're exchanging a longer, healthier life for what you gave up."

Across the room, Fuzzbucket yipped for Sky's attention. "How many pecks on the snout will it take before you learn to leave that old rooster alone?" she asked the poodle.

Max, the happy-faced German shepherd, sat calmly in his kennel cage, oblivious to the fact that in the morning, he'd share the cat's fate.

"Okay, kids," she announced, yawning, "lights out. C'mon, Face. Let's go to bed."

Sky was halfway between the clinic and the house when she noticed a shadow dart between two pines, causing their needled boughs to bounce lazily. "Stay, girl!" she ordered. Despite Face's low growls, Sky forced herself to keep moving at a steady pace, straining her eyes to see what had caused the movement. She'd grown accustomed to the occasional coyote or raccoon that ambled into her yard, but something told her that whatever lurked in the trees was far more omi-

nous and evil than any creature that called the woods home.
The eerie sensation suddenly became too much to bear with
respectable calm, and Sky bolted for the porch. Safe inside,
she breathed a sigh of relief. "Chet has me scared of my
own shadow," she said. Face woofed her agreement.

She lay awake for a long time, watching the clock's numbers change from 11:40 to 12:00 to 12:30. The wispy white
curtain rose and fell on the breeze that slipped through the
tiny opening she'd left in her bedroom window. It was well
after one o'clock before she finally drifted off to sleep.

At first, she thought it was helicopter blades chopping in
the distance, or soft jungle drum beats, or maybe the *thud-
thud-thud* of Face's paws padding across the braided rug in
the living room. Sleepily, Sky lifted her head from the pillow, trying to identify the sound that seemed to be coming
from just outside the window. "Footsteps…?"

Face whimpered as Sky tossed the covers aside and glanced
at the clock. It was only 3:34 in the morning. Wide awake
now, she tiptoed to the window in time to see a dark-clothed,
crouching figure running alongside the pines, precisely where
she'd seen the shadow earlier. In an instant, the shadow was
gone, swallowed up by the never-ending murk of darkness.

Soundlessly, she opened the nightstand drawer and withdrew her father's big black flashlight. She walked through
the hall and into the foyer, the unlit light resting on her shoulder like a baseball bat.

Sky stopped dead in her tracks and nearly collided with
Face when she saw the inky rectangle, silhouetted by moonlight, in the center of the front door's etched glass window.
Keeping her back to the wall, Sky sneaked closer. Holding
her breath, she peeked through the narrow, beveled pane beside the door. Satisfied no one was on the porch, she released
the dead bolt and cringed as it echoed in the wide, uncarpeted

space. Old brass hinges squealed mercilessly as she opened the heavy oak door. Quickly, she grabbed the note, slammed the door, and locked it tight.

Weak with fear, she slumped to the floor, her hands trembling violently as she held the scrap of paper under the flashlight's beam and read:

> *You're not fooling anyone. Get rid of them,*
> *or we'll do it for you.*
> > *Your neighbors*

six

Panic rose in Sky's throat as she read and reread the messy, maniacal handwriting: "Get rid of them, or we'll do it for you." Racing across the lawn, the note crumpled in the palm of her hand, she prayed he hadn't gotten to them. She tugged the padlock on the shelter's door. Amazingly, it was still locked tight. Her hands trembled as she shoved the key into the lock and, when she stepped inside, the cubs roused from a deep sleep and yawned. She'd taught them that bright light and warm words meant mealtime; anything else could be ignored. For a moment, their eyes, glowing red in the dim shaft of moonlight that spilled down the steps and into the underground room, blinked sleepily at her. Realizing she wasn't there to provide fun or food, they snuggled together once again, and closed their eyes. Satisfied with their safety, Sky relocked the doors and headed back to the house.

She was halfway between the shed and the house when she decided to call Dr. Williams. He'd been her guide and her inspiration as she'd prepared the Alaskan wolves for their return to the wild. Surely when she told him what was going on in Montana, he'd consent to take Piney and Rocky far away from Mountain Gate, Montana.

In the kitchen, Sky's hands trembled as she thumbed through her personal phone book, then dialed the long distance number. His phone rang once. Twice. The clock above the stove said 3:55; in Virginia, it was nearly six in the morning. Sky hoped he was still an early riser. A whiskey-voiced woman answered on the fourth ring, and Sky immediately apologized for calling so early. "Steven has retired due to ill health," the lady said. "He's not to be disturbed under any circumstances."

"Let me leave my name and number, then," Sky suggested, "and the professor can return my call at his convenience."

"I'm afraid that's impossible," she said. "Dr. Williams' family has hired me as his full-time nurse. He's had a stroke, you see, and can't speak with anyone." With that, she hung up.

Sky ran her hands through her hair and paced the brightly lit kitchen. *Nothing ventured,* she remembered. And once again, the motto proved itself worthy. Sky had shared two years with the elderly professor. What began as a teacher/student relationship became a strong friendship. If she had insisted on a working connection only, she'd be sorry now to hear of his illness, of course, but her heart wouldn't ache this way. *When will you ever learn!* she scolded herself.

Face, staring at the moon, visible through the uncurtained kitchen windows, whimpered. Suddenly, Sky remembered what Chet had said: "Someone with binoculars could watch from any direction." Her property, as he'd so astutely pointed out, sat in the middle of nowhere. Nestled in a gently sloping valley, her closest neighbors were of the Mother Nature variety: mountains, a canyon and a prairie, a thick pine forest—plenty of hiding places from every angle.

Sky shivered as she wandered through the house. Even curled up in a tiny ball beneath Gran's flowery afghan on the living room sofa, she couldn't relax, because every window in the house seemed like soulless black eyes, unblinking, watching her every move, never allowing her to see more than her own reflection. Before the wolf mess, Mountain Gate's very location had made it a haven. Now, it made her feel exposed and vulnerable. Sky rode an emotional seesaw, swinging between panic and rage. Panic that someone unknown could bring harm to her or the cubs; rage that his secrecy made her powerless to stop him.

Wide awake, Sky headed back into the kitchen. After she had tacked several towels over the windows, she began doing what she always did when sleep eluded her. Long ago she had memorized Gran's chocolate chip cookie recipe and she found that the mechanics of measuring and sifting and kneading would always calm her, no matter how upset she was. So, by the time the clock told her it was five in the morning, time to feed and exercise the cubs, she'd baked six batches of cookies.

The cubs greeted her with their customary damp kisses. "You guys give a whole new meaning to the term 'tongue lashing,'" she said, laughingly enduring their affections. Today she'd begin to teach them to howl, a chore she prayed she could accomplish.

She'd spent hours last week, sitting in the wilderness with her hand-held tape recorder, capturing the blood-curdling howls of the wolf pack that lived beyond the foothills. She'd spent considerable time, rubbed down thoroughly with creek slime to disguise her human scent, watching from her perch behind the thick brambles beyond the rocks.

She'd seen the black alpha male, huge and formidable, several times before. The first time though, she hadn't prepared herself with the creek disguise. A camera in one hand and her trusty backpack dangling from the other, Sky had been perched on a rock, hoping to catch a glimpse of the mountain goat family that often tiptoed up and down the steep incline that skirted the foothills near Magic Mountain. She sensed him before her eyes actually found him, standing majestically atop a rocky overhang above her.

The eye contact was at once eerie and satisfying; his golden gaze seemed to slide straight down inside her and nestle permanently in a place deep within her soul. Though only thirty yards separated her from the mighty beast, something in his demeanor told Sky she had nothing to fear. So she sat, motionless, fully intending to remain where she was for hours, if he'd allow it, reveling in his magnificence. Five minutes ticked silently by before he sat back on his haunches. Ten minutes later, he assumed the position of the Sphinx. But never in those moments did his all-knowing eyes leave her. Knowing that too much eye contact would be read as aggression, Sky occasionally lowered her eyes. Each time she looked at him again, he lifted his chin, as if to say, "Go ahead. Feast your eyes." Sky was so enjoying her studies that she grinned. The beast stood when she did and, much to her surprise, sent a doggy grin of his own down the mountainside.

Then suddenly, he left her, moving with the grace and power of an eagle. Sky decided to call him Raven. It was his pack she'd recorded that afternoon, and the next afternoon, too.

By now the cubs were eating only two meals a day. Sky pleasured in the fact, since it meant fewer trips to the shelter and less chance of being seen by the horrible Hidden Man, as she'd come to call him. Soon she'd face the difficult chore of feeding them only every third or fourth day. If she was to be successful at teaching them to hunt on their own, they'd have to be hungry. It didn't matter one bit to Sky that the measure was a necessary and important part of their survival training, since feast or famine was a natural and normal part of life in the wild. And it was little consolation that they'd received far better care and attention from her than they'd have gotten from their wolf pack. Refusing them anything, especially food, would be a difficult and heartbreaking thing.

Though the air was warm and the sky sunny on that fall morning, she didn't dare let the cubs outside to play in the fenced yard, and they protested loudly. She wondered exactly how she'd accomplish the hunting aspect of their outdoor education, when Hidden Man could take a potshot from any direction at any time. Sky decided to take the Scarlett O'Hara approach to that problem and worry about that when the time came.

The steak bones that Chet had brought back from the restaurant appeased the cubs for a while but, even before she'd finished cleaning up their newspaper mess, the pair were whimpering and scratching at the big metal door. "Sorry, guys," she said, drawing them into a hug, "can't let you out there 'til I'm sure it's safe." *And who knows how long that might be?* she wondered. Side by side, Piney and Rocky sat in the middle of their now-tattered old quilt, heads cocked and brows raised in canine confusion.

She turned on the recorder, hoping to distract them from their yearning to be outside. The moment the first howl echoed through the shelter, both cubs stood on all fours, ears keened toward the sound of their relatives. Piney was the first to react, her little mouth opening and closing as she tried to figure out how to duplicate that peculiar noise. But it was Rocky who cut loose with the first near howl that either cub would utter. It seemed to surprise him that he'd produced such a cry, and he jumped back. But the caterwauling that came from the black box made him forget his apprehension; male ego wouldn't allow him to be outsung by another being, and Rocky lifted his scraggly head. Eyes closed and mouth open wide, black dog lips covered his white teeth as the pink tongue lolled to the back of his throat. This time, his wail sent shivers down Sky's spine. With a little more practice, she knew, he'd have a howl as powerful as Raven's.

"What's the matter, Piney?" Sky said, ruffling her furry neck. "You jealous that your brother's one up on you?"

Piney made a habit of butting Sky, as if she thought herself a billy goat instead of a wolf. She butted Sky now, grumbling a low, playful growl. She paid no mind to the mournful howls coming from the recorder…and her brother.

"Don't you worry, girl," Sky said, hugging her. "Before you know it, you'll be hollering with the best of them."

Piney sat back on her haunches, panting, looking at Sky as if to say, "Only if I feel like it."

Sky glanced at her watch. She had surgery scheduled for eight-thirty. She hated to leave them, because being sequestered in the shelter, teaching them to behave like proper wolves, was the only real joy she derived from life these days. Down there in the cool, quiet, underground space, she could forget about notes and phone calls and loved ones lost. Sadly, she left them to play with their new toys, two teddy bears and a red rubber ball.

As she had baked cookies last night, Sky had decided that a business-as-usual attitude was safest, for now at least. The phone jangled as she walked into the clinic, and she hoped it wouldn't be Hidden Man.

"I was about to hang up," Chet said when she answered. "Is everything all right?"

It amazed her that the mere sound of his voice could provoke a smile on her face, even amid the cub turmoil on Magic Mountain. For a fleeting moment, she considered telling him about her terrifying, sleepless night. But Sky remembered how she'd called Dale in a moment of panic. If she asked for help again, it would only be after she'd given it a lot of careful thought.

"Everything is terrific," she blurted. "Why wouldn't it be?"

"I don't know. You sounded…odd when you answered."

"Probably because I took your advice and didn't let the cubs outside for their morning romp…in case someone might be watching. They cried like babies. Guess I'm a little down at seeing them so disappointed."

His soft laugh filtered into her ear. "Look at it this way: At least they're alive to *be* disappointed."

Silently, she agreed.

"What are you doing for lunch?"

Sky glanced at the clock. It wasn't even eight o'clock yet. "I have surgery in half an hour, and back-to-back appointments from nine 'til eleven. Why?"

"I promised Sally I'd take her to Big Jim's. It'd be a good way for you two to meet."

When he'd shown her Sally's picture at dinner, Sky said she'd like to meet his little girl someday. But the very next day? The note crinkled in her pocket and Sky hesitated, afraid for a moment to leave the clinic and the house vulnerable to the Hidden Man. Then she remembered the promise she'd made to herself last night, when she was elbow deep in flour: She wouldn't give him the satisfaction of knowing he'd terrorized her. Sky intended to live life as normally as possible, to make him wonder whether she'd received his message at all. *Let him see that through his binoculars!* she thought.

"So what do you say?" Chet asked. "Can I pick you up at noon?"

Sky loved his musical, masculine voice. *Too bad the singing doesn't come out sounding as melodious,* she thought, grinning as she remembered the way he'd harmonized with Willie Nelson. "I guess I can be out of my scrubs and into jeans by then."

"Time's gonna drag 'til twelve," he said, and hung up.

seven

Chet and Sally arrived ten minutes early and Sky was still buckling her belt when the doorbell rang. She hurried down the long hall that ran the length of her ranch-style house, paused in front of the foyer mirror, and fluffed her hair. Smiling, she opened the door wide. "Come on in."

Chet stood on the porch, wearing a crisp white shirt and black trousers, looking handsome as ever. Grinning, he said, "You look...rested."

Her smile faded slightly as she closed the door behind him. She hadn't told him she'd been up all night, worrying about the shadow in the pines and the note she'd found taped to her door. And she hadn't told him she'd been baking like a maniac. Again, a horrible suspicious sensation crowded her mind. "Why wouldn't I look rested?"

Chet only shrugged. "Sally, this is Dr. Allen. Sky, I'd like you to meet the love of my life."

"Pleased to meet you," Sally said. "I smell chocolate chip cookies."

Just as Martha had said, Sally was an exact replica of Ella, from her sparkling blue eyes to her honey blond hair and ballerina-like frame. Warm summer days of hide-and-seek, picnics, and Barbie trade-offs flashed through her memory, and Sky wanted to wrap the child in a bear hug. Instead, she smiled. "As a matter of fact, I baked some last night. Would you like one?"

Sally nodded, causing her golden ponytails to bob up and down. "Chocolate chips are my favorite," she said, following Sky into the kitchen. "Oh, my," she said, entering the room, "it's a cookie factory!"

Chet's gray eyes scanned the stovetop, the counters, the table and chairs. "Is there a place in here that *isn't* covered with cookies?"

Sally giggled and pointed at the trash can. "There's one!" Following Sally's pointer finger, Sky noticed the note, lying in a crumpled ball on the floor near the trash can. She laughed.

"I get a little carried away when I bake." She'd angrily pitched the note into the trash can earlier; obviously, she'd missed. Quickly, she scooped it up. "I don't think your dad will mind if you have just one cookie before lunch," Sky said, nonchalantly stuffing the note into the garbage can before Chet had a chance to see it.

"Okay," he said in response to Sally's imploring eyes, "one cookie. But then we'd better get a move on. You know how crowded Big Jim's gets at high noon."

Sally tugged Chet's hand and, when he bent down, she whispered loudly into his ear, "You're right, Daddy; she's very tall and very pretty." To Sky, she said, "Are you really a dog doctor?"

Sky smiled. "Yes, and a cat doctor, and a cow doctor, and a horse doctor, too." She studied the child's face for a moment, then added, "Maybe you'd like to see the clinic when we get back from lunch."

The ponytails bobbed again. "Can Daddy come, too?" Sky met Chet's eyes. "Well, maybe if he promises to stay out of our way...."

He seemed to be sending a silent, secret message by way of those crystalline gray eyes, and Sky wished for the power to read it. Then he blinked, ending the trancelike connection, and looked at his watch. "Is everybody ready for burgers and fries?"

Sally knew dozens of knock-knock jokes, and told them all, making Sky wonder if bad joke telling was an inheritable trait. As Chet munched his steak sandwich and Sky her salad, Sally offered them french fries from her kid's meal.

Later, while she romped in the children's playroom among monkey bars and soft colorful balls, he barely took his eyes off her.

"She's something, isn't she?" Chet asked.

"She's adorable," Sky agreed. "It's easy to see why you're so proud of her."

He met Sky's eyes. "It's not pride. At least, that's not all it is. It's…. Sally's all I have."

She considered pointing out that he had more, so much more. He owned one of the largest cattle ranches in the state. Lived in an historic manor house. Had the love and respect of friends, relatives, and employees. He was robustly healthy, despite his limp, and enormously good looking, to boot. But he believed his little girl was his only connection to a happy past. The house, the ranch, the money…it was all worthless without Sally. Sky realized that behind Chet's tough-guy exterior beat the heart of a man who melted at the mere sight of one, tiny blond.

"Until my dad was killed," she said softly, "I thought I had the world on a stick. My very own big blue lollipop. The world just isn't the same without him. But it's still spinning just as fast."

He gazed at her for a long time and Sky wondered what sad thoughts had dimmed the life spark in those gleaming gray eyes. "Is there any particular time you need to get back to the clinic?"

In response to his formal tone of voice, she said, "Why do you ask, Mr. Cozart?"

Sally skipped up to the table just then. "You don't have to call him Mr. Cozart," she said, one hand on Sky's arm. "You can call him Chester if you want."

Sky tried to meet his eyes, which he'd hidden behind a large work-hardened hand. "Chester?"

Sally slid into the booth beside Sky. "Dale and Grandfather call him Chet, but Grandmother calls him Chester. That's his real name. Isn't that right, Daddy?"

Chet sighed and came out of hiding. Shaking his head and grinning, he looked from Sky to his daughter and back again. "That's right, honey." Nodding, and wearing a silly, tight-lipped grin, he patted Sky's hand. "Please. Call me Chet. All my friends do."

So. He'd added her name to his "Friends" list. Sky took one last sip of her soda, then busied herself by gathering burger wrappers and french fry cartons on the red plastic tray in the middle of their table. She didn't quite know how to react to being included in that exclusive circle.

Sky had been looking at Sally and, when she looked up, she realized Chet had been looking at *her*.

"What do you say we bring Dr. Allen home to meet Tootsie?" he asked, never taking his eyes from Sky's.

The child clasped her hands together and beamed. "Would you like that, Dr. Allen?"

Sky couldn't help it; she was doing a lot of beaming of her own lately, it seemed. "Sounds like a great idea."

❧

Driving to Four Aces Ranch, Sally chattered about her horse. She'd gotten her for Christmas last year, she said, when her daddy bought himself the new car. "She's very big, but very gentle," Sally said. "Daddy lets me ride her alone, when he rides Sugar."

In the barn, perched on the stall's gate, she brushed Tootsie's mane. "Do you know how she got her name, Dr. Allen?"

Sky squinted at the mare, and gave the matter some serious thought. "Because she's the same color as a Tootsie Roll?"

Sally's wide eyes swung toward Chet, who held the waist os his precariously-balanced child. "She's smart, too, Daddy."

"Mm-mmm. And brave," he added, his eyes boring hotly into Sky's. "Too brave for her own good sometimes, I'm afraid."

Sally, busy with her horse's hairdo, paid the adults' conversation no mind. But Sky's brown eyes darkened at Chet's obvious wolf reference. She glanced at her watch. They'd been at Four Aces less than ten minutes and already she felt trapped.

"You know, I just remembered that today is Lisa's early day," she said the first thing that came to her mind, "and Cuddles will be needing some one-on-one."

"Who's Cuddles?" Sally wanted to know.

"He's a cat. He had an operation this morning, so he's not feeling very well right now."

Sally wrapped her arms around Chet's neck and said, "You'd better take her right home. She has 'portant work to do."

"Sometimes you're smarter than your old dad, kiddo," he said, putting her gently on the hay-covered floor.

"Is it two o'clock yet?"

"Fifteen minutes before."

"Oh no!" she shouted, both hands over her mouth. "I'll be late for my riding lesson!"

"You won't be late, sweetie. Run on up to the house and take off that pretty dress. Then ask Grandmother if she'll help you find your riding clothes. Now, give us a great big kiss." Chet squatted and held out his arms. Sally fell into them and pressed a loud kiss on his cheek.

In the doorway, she stopped. "Dr. Allen, can I visit the animal hospital tomorrow, since we didn't have time today?"

She looked at Chet but, unable to read his mood, said, "If it's all right with your dad, it's fine with me."

In response to the child's unasked question, Chet said, "I think we can squeeze in a few minutes."

Waving, Sally ran toward the mansion. "See you tomorrow, Dr. Allen," she called over her shoulder.

Sky grinned. "How old is she, Chet? Twenty-four, twenty-five?"

"Almost five," he said, laughing. "Bright as a new penny, isn't she?"

"Takes after her dad in that department."

He shoved both hands into his pockets and flushed like a schoolboy. "Well, she's the spitting image of her mother in every other way. Sometimes when I look at her," he said, staring after her, "I see Ella looking back at me. It's...." Chet shook his head, as if to shake off a painful memory. "I think you must be part psychiatrist; you have a way of making me tell you things I've never told any...." He took a deep breath. "Guess we'd better get you home before your assistant turns into a pumpkin."

Impulsively, she grabbed his hand and squeezed it gently. "Sally does look a lot like her mother. And I'm glad, because she reminds me of all the good times Ella and I had when we were kids." Sky's cheeks flushed and tears stung her eyes. "When I lost my dad, I couldn't come back here; the place was nothing but memories of him. I never realized until today how much more I lost by staying away."

Chet stared at the hay-strewn floor.

She squeezed his hand again. "Listen to me, Chet; memories are all I have of my dad, but you have Sally to help you remember Ella. That shouldn't make you sad."

He met her eyes for an instant and, in that instant, Sky saw those long, black lashes blink away unshed tears. He coughed, then looked toward the door. "It doesn't make me sad," he said, an angry edge to his voice. "The good Lord's seen fit to bless me with that little angel, and I'm thankful every day of my life for her." He sighed deeply, then added, "Guess we'd better go."

Eleven miles separated Four Aces and Magic Mountain and they drove five without speaking. He stayed busy playing with the radio dials and the rearview mirror. Every now and then, he'd open his mouth, as if to say something, then quickly close it. Finally, he said, "When were you planning to tell me about the note, Sky?"

eight

Sky had been staring out the window, amazed that the sky and the cattle and the trees looked as bright from inside the black-windowed truck as they did outside. "What note?"

Chet's right hand slapped the steering wheel. "The one Dale told me about. The one somebody delivered while sneaking around your place in the middle of the night." He shot her a wary look. "Why? Have there been others?"

Dale, Sky thought, *needs to learn to keep his big yap shut.* "It was one note. Dale's making mountains out of molehills, as usual. It's awfully close to Halloween. I'm sure it's just a silly, teenage prank."

Sighing loudly, Chet turned off the radio. "You seem to have a mental block where this wolf stuff is concerned. I wish I could get it through your head that you're in real danger."

Sky smoothed the creases in her jeans. "I'm beginning to sound like a broken record, I know, but I'm going to say it again: The cubs have no one but me. So, dangerous or not, I'll take my chances. Besides, it's too late to back out now."

"If I've learned one thing in life, it's that it's never too late."

"But if I release them, your bounty hunters will—"

Slapping the steering wheel again, he shouted, "Sky! Why do you insist on calling them *my* bounty hunters? I had nothing to do with that bounty!"

"It's *your* ranch. You could—"

"That's right. It's my ranch," he interrupted, "and I'll run

74

it any way I see fit. And if I see fit to let an old man hold onto what little pride he's got left, then that's what I intend to do."

"At what cost?"

A thick cloud of dust swirled around them as he brought the truck to a jerking halt on the side of the road. "What is that supposed to mean?" he demanded, turning off the motor.

"You allow poor old Bud to play boss, and everybody suffers. The cubs, me,...."

Chet leaned his forehead against his hands, which tightly gripped the steering wheel. After muttering a string of unintelligible words under his breath, he turned sideways on the bench seat. "There's no getting through to you, is there? How will I ever make you understand?"

Sky focused, for a moment, on the padded ceiling of his truck, then sighed. "I understand perfectly. Half-breed wolves have attacked some cattle, because they're not terrified of humans, like the purebreds are. And the ranchers are reacting by shooting every wolf on sight, half-breed *and* purebred, in the middle of a meal or not. I don't have to agree with their vigilante mentality to understand it!"

She turned in the seat, too, so that they faced one another squarely. "What I have in my shelter are *cubs*. They couldn't take down a steer if they tried."

Chet only stared at her.

Feeling helpless, she raised her hands, then dropped them into her lap. "I know the cubs are hybrids, that they'll very likely wander from the foothills, looking for easy pickings in a herd of cattle when they're grown. If they're struck by lightning or attacked by a moose or shot by a bounty hunter, well, that's nature's way. But they deserve a fighting chance. That's all I'm trying to give them...a fighting chance."

He took her hands in his. "But not everybody out there," he nodded toward the rolling acres beyond the windshield, "can afford your mindset. Expect the worst, then do everything you can to prevent it. Weather, coyotes, rustlers…it's a code ranchers have learned to live with."

Sky couldn't look into those dark-lashed steely eyes a moment longer, afraid they had the power to convince her to turn the cubs loose, after all. She focused on their hands. This hand-holding thing had become a pattern and she wondered exactly how it got started.

Chet took a deep breath, let go of her, and started the motor. They drove the remaining six miles to Magic Mountain without even the radio to distract them from their separate yet similar thoughts.

Sky watched his jaw flex in anger and, when he parked in her driveway, she half expected him to plant the sole of his cowboy boot in the middle of her back and shove her out onto the gravel. Instead, he walked around to her side of the truck and, with all the decorum of a proper English butler, opened her door.

"I want to see that note," he said before her feet hit the ground.

It wasn't a request. She almost told him to get lost, to butt out, to mind his own business, once and for all. But despite all outward appearances of bravado, the note and the way it had been delivered had frightened her terribly. If she showed it to Chet, maybe he'd recognize the handwriting and the whole sorry mess would be over and done with before nightfall.

Sky unlocked the front door and invited him to wait in the foyer. "I'm going over to the clinic to tell Lisa she can lock up and go home. The note is in the kitchen," she said, leaving him alone on the porch.

"I know exactly where it is," he called after her. "In the trash can. Right where you put it. My leg doesn't work like it used to, but there's nothin' wrong with my eyes."

That made her giggle, because she believed she'd retrieved that note and disposed of it smoothly. *Not smoothly enough to fool the likes of Chester Cozart,* she told herself.

When she returned, he was clearing a space for them at the cookie covered kitchen table. "Okay, so let's see it," he said around a mouthful of chocolate chip.

Grinning, she held back the swinging trash can lid, retracted the note, and handed it to him. "I thought you said you knew exactly where it was."

"I don't make a habit of digging through other people's garbage." He snatched the note from her, read it, then read it again. "Now, here's a friendly greeting if ever I saw one."

"Would you like some coffee to wash down that cookie?" she asked, ignoring his mockery.

Chet threw his hands into the air. "No, Sky. I wouldn't like some coffee to wash down this cookie. What I want is for you to tell me how you plan to accomplish this spectacular cub-rearing feat without getting yourself killed!"

She willed her lower lip to stop trembling. When it wouldn't obey, she bit it—hard.

"Look," he said, crossing the room to where her backside leaned against the sink, "it's obvious I was right." He waved the note in the air. "You're in big trouble. You could get hurt. There's no point denying it. Like it or not, you've got to get rid of those animals."

She looked up at him. The stern yet compassionate light in his eyes made her remember how safe she'd felt in his arms last night and how disappointed she'd been when he left without giving her a chance to discover what that wonderful, mustachioed mouth might feel like against her lips. *You're very close to losing it, Sky, old girl.*

He must have read her mind, for Chet wrinkled the note and tossed it over his shoulder. "Something is happening here," he whispered, stepping closer and lifting her chin, "and I don't know whether to run from it, or straight at it."

Sky trembled as his muscular body pinned her to the cabinet. She inhaled crisp aftershave and his sweet cookie breath. *Nothing ventured, nothing lost,* she thought. *Nothing ventured, nothing....*

Chet groaned. "Oh, why not."

When his lips touched hers, Sky gasped. The soul-stirring taste of him sent silent shockwaves straight to her heart. Weak-kneed and lightheaded, she felt his arms encircle her, providing sure-footed and much-needed support. Slowly, his fingers combed through her hair, traced down her shoulders and her back, gently caressed her cheeks as the mustache she'd been so curious about skimmed, light as a feather, from her earlobes to her throat to her forehead, leaving a sizzling trail in its wake before sliding back to her slightly parted, waiting lips.

Between kisses, he stammered and stuttered, and his words made no sense to her. "It's been...never thought I'd...so long since...Sky," he sighed. "Sky...."

When Chet said it, her name was a soft spring breeze, rustling the pines and sending dogwood petals floating gently through the air. Liking the way he'd warmed her lonely heart, she wanted to learn more about this strong-willed man—until her life's motto sliced the moment short.

He seemed to sense her sudden mood swing and he gradually ended the delicious kiss. "I don't know what's gotten into me," he murmured shakily near her ear, still holding her close. Then, looking long and deep into her eyes, he added, "That's a lie. I know exactly what's gotten into me."

A tightrope walker could have balanced on the taut thread that melded their eyes. Chet stood back slightly, his eyes sliding over her features, reminding Sky where his lips had been just seconds ago. She waited for him to tell her exactly what had gotten into him.

"I sure could use that cup of coffee now," he said instead.

Small talk over the chocolate chip cookie mountain was companionable, as it had been on her porch, at the restaurant, at Big Jim's, in his barn. When Chet stood to leave, she wanted to stop him. She wanted to feel his big, protective arms around her, making her forget the horrible, frightening wolf-related threats. She wanted him to prove to her that her life's motto was a worthless, silly cliché and nothing more. "Wait."

He'd stacked cookies as they talked, and now he was straightening the teetering columns he'd made. "Wait?"

Sky thought he seemed pleased, even happy, that she wanted him to stay. "Just let me pack up some cookies...for Sally."

He grinned. "Do you do this often?" His big hand waved over the cookie pile.

"Only when I'm upset. Baking soothes me."

Chet chuckled softly. "From the looks of things, that note must have upset you a lot."

Sky was stuffing a small grocery sack with the sweet treats when he bent over to pick up the note. It seemed to have developed a life of its own, appearing and disappearing, flaunting its threat at its whim. Chet stuffed it into his shirt pocket and patted it. "Never know when it might come in handy...as evidence."

Her hands froze above the bag. "Evidence? Evidence of what?"

Shrugging, he said, "Don't know. But it's better to be safe than sorry, I say."

Sky clutched the bag tightly as her heart raced.

"Aw, c'mon now," he said. "Don't look like that." He hugged her and a cookie crumbled inside the bag, which he'd pinned between them. "I didn't mean to scare you," he said, kissing her forehead. "It's just that my tongue wags like an old woman's when I'm around you. There's an old Indian legend that says some women can cast spells. I'm beginning to believe you've cast one on me."

"Mm-mm," she said, calmer already, now that she stood in the warm circle of his embrace. "It's my favorite hex: Eye of newt, male tongue loosed," she chanted.

Laughter, deep in his chest, rumbled against her. "I'd better get home before Sally calls the sheriff and reports me missing."

He took her hand. "Walk me to the door." In the foyer, he said, "I'm as near as the phone. You know that, right?" Then, before she had a chance to agree, or tell him she could take care of herself, or ask him not to go, he clutched her to him and kissed the top of her head.

Sky had never really been in love before, but suspected that that was exactly what had been going on inside her heart and her head and her soul ever since she'd met Chet. She couldn't afford such a huge distraction right now, however pleasant it might be.

"Lock up tight. You hear?"

Nodding against his hard chest, Sky wondered if he'd kiss her goodbye. Because if he did, she intended to respond entirely differently than she had earlier in the kitchen. This time, she'd be sophisticated, reserved. Anything else, and she may as well throw her life's motto out the window. Much to her disappointment, he didn't put her to the test.

🍂

Chet had been gone nearly an hour before she finished cleaning up the evidence of her baking frenzy. As she scrubbed cookie sheets, Sky hoped the note writer had poked around long enough to have convinced himself that no wolf cubs lived on Magic Mountain. The shelter was soundproof; he couldn't possibly have heard them as he prowled. And, unless he'd seen them from a distance while she exercised them in the fenced yard, as Chet had suggested, the vile man had only left the note on a hunch, as a warning of what might happen if she didn't comply with his demands.

Sky forced the horrid thought out of her mind and rummaged through the cupboards for containers in which to store the cookies. Like a ghost, the memory of Chet's kiss followed her every move. She floated on that cloud of blissful remembrance until every cookie, except for one plateful that sat in the middle of the table, was sealed up tightly.

She was sweeping cookie crumbs from the black-and-white tiled floor when the idea first struck. Sky hated her suspicious mind as it wondered if perhaps Chet had pocketed the note to protect *himself.*

She stood, stock-still in the middle of the floor, gripping the broom handle like a protective weapon. *Chet's a wealthy man*, her heart said. *Certainly he doesn't need the bounty money. Still, he always seems to show up in conjunction with some frightening event,* insisted her brain. *But he's part Cheyenne*, her heart argued, *and he respects all things in nature.*

Picturing his slanting, black-lashed eyes, she remembered the romantic scene in the kitchen. Distractedly, she began sweeping again. Her instincts told her that Chet had nothing to do with the terrifying phone calls and the threatening note. No man who'd done what Chet had done for Pablo and Bud, who'd been the kind of daddy he'd been to Sally, could threaten a woman one minute, and kiss the living daylights out of her the next.

As she dumped the dustpan of cookie crumbs into the trash can, the battle between her heart and her brain ended, but she sensed that the war was far from over.

nine

Sky spent the night tossing and turning. As a child, Gran had taught her that prayer and reciting Bible verses could make almost any situation seem minor. But not even repeating the Twenty-third Psalm calmed her enough to get that vicious note out of her mind. Long before the alarm clock sounded, she'd dressed and headed for the shelter. The extra two hours with the cubs would do them all a lot of good. Every day, they grew more restless with their cramped quarters, prowling and growling and behaving like caged zoo animals. Sky knew she had to get them out of there, fast. But how, with the Hidden Man lurking out there…somewhere?

She decided to wait until nightfall, then sneak on foot into Beartooth country. She believed the cubs would stay close to her, since they thought of her as their mother. She'd learned some low growling tones of her own, watching the wolf pack from her hiding place in the trees, then mimicking the mother wolves' behavior and calls. So far, her attempts at sounding wolflike had been effective in keeping them in line…at least in the shelter. Whether or not they'd be as obedient in their own element remained to be seen. But Sky had no choice but to give it a try. "Tonight's the night," she announced when she entered the shelter.

Face, Piney, and Rocky picked up on her excitement, howling and woofing and running small circles around their "mom." She'd take them to her favorite spot, high in canyon country, where she and Wade had gone so many times. The cubs would have an opportunity to commune with nature there, and the likelihood of their tormenter following or finding them was slim.

Since there were no appointments scheduled for the day, Sky decided to give the clinic a thorough cleaning. That done, she rearranged and organized her files. She'd skipped breakfast and lunch, and her stomach growled as she walked into the house. The red blinking light of her answering machine told her she'd received three calls. Her heart skipped a beat as she pressed the rewind button. "Maybe your pal called," she said to Face. "Wouldn't that be nice?"

Wagging her tail, the dog barked.

"Dr. Allen?"

Immediately, Sky recognized the intimidating drawl. She grabbed the answering machine with both hands and pulled it closer on the desktop. "We've just about run out of patience with you. You've got 'til Sunday to turn those wolves loose." One second...two seconds hissed by before his grating voice again said, "Sunday."

Sky dropped into the chair, trembling as she depressed the rewind button and listened for the end-of-message *beep*. *Why is his voice so familiar?* she demanded. The answer had better come soon, she knew, because with each threat, he grew bolder and more brazen. Sky couldn't imagine why he'd give her this second piece of physical evidence. Was he that stupid? Or simply that sure he could carry out his threats without getting caught? Sky shuddered at the thought.

She listened to the message four more times, hoping to match a name or a face with the horrible voice. Finally, when the haunting voice was no more recognizable than before, she let the tape play itself out.

Once the *scribble-squeal* of the rewinding tape ended, Sky hit the save button and held her head in her hands, unable to concentrate on anything but the tiny red light, blinking on and off. She could have sworn the first flash—his message—lasted longer and blinked brighter than the other two. Sky was about to add the old tape to the strongbox when the phone rang, scaring her so badly she nearly leaped out of the chair. When it shrilled a second time, she prayed, *Don't let it be him.*

"Animal Clinic," she said into the mouthpiece of the phone.

"Dr. Allen?"

"Sally?" Sky couldn't imagine why the child would be calling her, especially in tears.

Sally cried harder. "Oh, Dr. Allen…Tootsie's bleeding. I don't want Tootsie to die…."

In the background, Sky heard Chet's patient yet authoritative voice. "Give Daddy the phone, sweetie." Several thumps and bumps later, he said, "We were out riding, and her horse got tangled in some barbed wire. I've stitched up stuff like this dozens of times, but Sally won't have anyone but you touch Tootsie." He paused. "I don't know who's more hysterical, Tootsie or Sally."

"Immobilize that animal any way you can," Sky instructed. "Tie her up if you have to. I'm on my way."

Sky called the owners of the two pets she was to inoculate that afternoon, explained the situation, and promised to reschedule their appointments soon. She flung back the supply cabinet door and stuffed sutures, gauze, a powerful tranquilizer, and a hypodermic of antibiotic into her medical bag, then ran out of the clinic, stopping only to lock the door.

Face had seen this flurry of activity before. Bored with the high tension atmosphere, she ran around to the backyard and climbed into her dog house.

On the clinic porch, Sky saw the answering machine through the slats of the mini-blinded window, its winking red light sending a last, taunting reminder. But Sky couldn't let herself dwell on that right now. She'd never shirked duty in her life, and didn't intend to start now. Speeding toward Four Aces, Sky wished she'd taken Gran's advice years ago and read Norman Vincent Peale's book. *The power of positive thinking would be pretty good medicine right about now,* she told herself.

The tree-lined driveway of Four Aces Ranch ribboned from the road to the five-car garage, then forked toward the barn. Sky brought the truck to a screeching halt as she saw Dale heading her way. "Chet's got her bandaged up fairly well," Dale said, running alongside her, "but we're having a time keeping her still. She's in the first stall," he added as they burst through the double doors.

Four pairs of eyes greeted her: Bud's, wary and stern; Sally's, brimming with tears; Stella's, distant and haughty; and Chet's, filled with concern.

Sky barged into the stall and dropped her medical bag, dodging Tootsie's high-kicking, pounding hooves. With one deft movement, she grabbed the horse's reins, wrapped the leather twice around her hand, and yanked. "I've got her," she told Dale. "The fewer people in here, the better." Once he'd moved to the outside of the stall's wall, Sky said in a strong, steady voice, "C'mon, now, Tootsie; calm down so I can have a look at that cut."

The horse had worked itself into such a frenzy, she'd all but kicked off the bandage Chet had so carefully applied, and the whites of her eyes were visible around the entire perimeter of chocolate brown iris.

Though Dale stood by, ready to assist her, it was Chet's eyes she sought out. "Looks like she's nearly severed an artery," she said, patting the horse's sweaty shoulder. "I'm going to need you."

Immediately, Chet stood beside her. "This doesn't look

good," he whispered. "Not good at all. We could lose her."

Sky smiled slightly. "Maybe not."

He picked up her medical bag, and held it out to Sky, but focused on his little girl. Sky didn't follow his gaze, because she couldn't bear to see the child's tear-streaked, heartbroken face again so soon. Sky maintained her firm grip on the horse's reins and continued to stroke her mane. Her quiet, in charge voice had at least slowed the horse's whinnying and stamping, but she knew better than to let go now. Continuity and speed were of the essence.

"There's a hypodermic in there," she told Chet, nodding toward the bag. She knew that most ranchers had to be part pet owner, part salesman, part farmer, part vet. Distance, lack of money…there were dozens of reasons they needed to wear so many hats.

"Have you ever given an injection before?" Sky asked.

Chet had been searching for the needle in the bag, and looked up quickly in response to her question. "Sure. Plenty of times. Why?"

"Because if I let go now, there's no telling how long it'll take to calm her down again. It's the white hypodermic with the blue label."

"Is Tootsie going to die, Daddy?"

Sky said, "Maybe you ought to hold Grandma's hand, Sally, so she won't be so scared."

In response to Sky's not-so-veiled hint, Stella's icy glare turned hatefully hot. But Sky refused to look away until she saw the woman take her granddaughter's hand.

Chet's position, facing the stall's back wall, helped hide his half-grin from his former mother-in-law, but not from Sky. In less time than it takes to blink, he'd sent an "atta girl" message her way and, despite the tenseness of the moment, Sky's heart fluttered. Then, as if he'd been doing it a lifetime, he removed the needle's protective cap. When it fell to the floor, he held the hypodermic in midair. "Ready when you are." He met her eyes, tucked in one corner of his mouth, took a deep breath, and did the deed. After he'd withdrawn the needle, he looked at Sky and grinned.

Sky smiled, too. "Good job."

Almost immediately, Tootsie began to relax. Sky turned to Dale. "C'mere and help us guide her to the floor."

That done, Sky gently removed what remained of the bandage that Chet had wound around the injury. Upon closer inspection, Sky saw that the barbs had nearly sliced to the bone. "Take Sally outside," she told Chet. "In fact, get everybody out of here. We've got to keep her calm, and we can't do that with a big audience." More for Stella's benefit than anything else, she added, "Besides, this could get messy." Then, unceremoniously, she poured isopropyl alcohol over her hands.

By the time he reached his daughter, she'd threaded the needle. Without looking up from her work, she knew that no one had made any move to leave the barn. She said in a stronger voice, "I mean it, Chet. Get them out of here. Now!"

"Well, I never!" she heard Stella say.

"It's my barn!" Bud added.

"But Grandmother! My teacher says we should always do what the doctor says," Sally announced, sniffing.

From the mouths of babes, Sky thought as Chet's former in-laws stomped out of the barn.

"We'll be in the kitchen," Stella said to Chet. "Come, Sally. Let's leave the animal doctor here in the barn...." Under her breath, but loud enough for Sky to hear, she added, "where she belongs."

Once Sally and her grandparents were gone, Dale snickered. "Shoo-eee! I haven't seen her that mad since we were fourteen and broke the terrace window. You could freeze a side of beef on that lady's stare."

Chet grinned and shook his head. "I'll say one thing for you, Sky. You sure know how to win friends and influence people."

Despite the seriousness of the moment, she smiled thinly. "I can take just about anything from anybody," she said, taking another stitch, "but I can't stand a person who thinks she's better than everybody else."

"Believe it or not," Chet said, "she's got a heart as big as Montana. Trouble is, she won't show it to anybody but family."

Sky admired his loyalty, even if she didn't agree with it. But Stella's character was quickly forgotten as she got to the business of repairing the horse's leg. It took nearly half an hour to complete the intricate patchwork. When Sky finished, Tootsie snorted softly and lifted her head.

Instinctively, Dale stroked her long, white-streaked nose. "It's okay, girl. You're in good hands."

"The best," Chet added.

Sky blushed, but hid it by digging in her doctor's bag.

Dale whistled. "I thought old Tootsie here was a goner for sure, the way she was bleeding. I've seen Chet sew up plenty cuts, but not the way you stitched up that one." He gave her a sideways hug and kissed her cheek. "Now I'm sorry I cancelled our date. I'd rather spend the evening with a hero than a pretty blond any day."

Chet's eyes went from rainy day to stormy skies gray. "You guys are…dating?"

Dale laughed. "You've gotta be kidding. We're like siblings." He ruffled her hair. "Right, sis?"

Playfully, she poked him in the ribs. "Yeah, well, you owe me dinner and a movie…bro'." Smiling, Sky couldn't help but wonder if the merry gleam had returned to Chet's eyes in response to the friends' teasing, or because it relieved him to learn she and Dale weren't a twosome.

"I've had to put down animals that were hurt as bad," Chet said. "You really think she'll be all right?"

"She won't be jumping any fences in her future, but she'll live."

"Sally's going to be relieved."

"Yeah. Sally," Dale said, chuckling as he lightly punched Chet's shoulder. "And her daddy wasn't sweating worry bullets in there ten minutes ago...."

Chet's left brow did its rising act. "'I'll thank you to keep your mitts to yourself, cowboy,'" he quoted, reminding Sky of the day they met. For the moment, they had eyes only for each other.

Dale looked from Sky to Chet and back again. "Okay. I'm outta here. A brick doesn't have to fall on my head." Walking backward toward the door, he added, "I know when I'm not wanted. I'll just leave you two lovebirds alone."

Neither Chet nor Sky seemed to notice if Dale had left or not. He took her hands in his own. "Dale's right. I've done patch jobs before, but not like that one. You did a terrific job in there," he said, looking from her bloodied fingers to her shining brown eyes. "Makes me right proud to be your... friend."

His arms slipped around her waist and he drew her to him. As his lips met hers, Tootsie struggled to her feet with a *clip* and a *clop* and a mighty puff of air, but neither Chet nor Sky seemed to notice.

"Where was Dale supposed to take you on this so-called date of yours tonight?"

Sky shrugged. With his lips still this close to hers, she couldn't think of much else, even her best friend. "It was his turn to pay; he's usually good for a burger and fries."

"How would you feel about another trip into Livingston?"

I'd feel like I'd died and gone to heaven. Her secret thought shocked her. *What kind of woman are you, Sky Allen,* she asked herself, *to have gone and fallen in love with your dead friend's husband? And what happened to your life's motto?* "Face is home alone, and I left so fast I didn't even put fresh water in her bowl. Besides, I have to—"

"Take care of the cubs," he droned.

Sky turned away from the disappointed look in his eyes and stepped out of his nourishing embrace. "Is she an evening feeder?" she asked, petting Tootsie's nose.

Chet pocketed his hands. "Morning. Why?"

"Good. She won't need to miss a meal."

"How long 'til your canines finish theirs?"

Sky's brows rose in confusion.

"Pablo serves dinner 'til eleven…."

She'd intended to keep the frightening messages on the clinic answering machine a secret, more determined than ever to display an everything's-normal façade. Going to Livingston would underscore that things were fine on Magic Mountain. Still, Sky couldn't bring herself to leave the house…and cubs… unprotected.

But his invitation moved her. She enjoyed his company… and everything that came with it. Sky had no explanation for the feelings bubbling inside her; she only knew that she felt happy and whole when she was with Chet. "Are you any good with charcoal and a fire?" she asked.

It was his turn to look puzzled.

"I took a pound of hamburger out of the freezer this morning; I couldn't possibly eat it all by myself. I could whip us up a bowl of potato salad, and you could put some burgers on Gramps' brick oven."

He grinned and led her out of the stall. "Just tell me what time to fire up the coals."

Sky glanced at her watch. "How's six sound? And bring Sally; it'll get her mind off Tootsie."

Unpocketing one hand, he grasped a wayward red curl. "I hate mustard in my potato salad."

Wrinkling her nose, she said, "Me, too."

Chet walked her to the truck and leaned into the opened window as she cranked up the motor. His nose was no more than an inch from hers and those gray eyes bore hotly into hers.

Sky wanted to run her fingers through his softly shining hair. To kiss that worried look off his handsome face. Instead, she contented herself with inhaling the masculine scent of fresh hay and hard work.

"Can I bring anything?"

"Just Sally," she said, shifting into reverse. "See you soon."

"Soon," he whispered, and kissed her cheek. His lips lingered longer than necessary, making what should have been an ordinary goodbye very memorable.

ten

When Chet and Sally arrived, characteristically fifteen minutes early, Chet carried a bag of charcoal under one arm and held a bouquet of white daisies in his free hand. "Sally's idea," he said, handing her the flowers.

Sky took the child's hand and smiled. "Thanks, little one," she said. "Daisies are my favorite flowers. How did you know?"

Sally grinned and looked at their hands. "Grandfather said Mommy loved daisies. And Daddy said you and Mommy were best friends. Best friends like the same things lots of the time." She shrugged her tiny shoulders and held her hands out, palms up. "That's how I knew."

She'd been wanting to hug this kid since the first time she set eyes on her. The spur-of-the-moment gesture didn't seem to surprise Sally at all. The child hugged Sky's neck with a power that belied her size. "Thanks, little one," Sky said.

"You're welcome. Are there any chocolate chip cookies left?"

As Sally munched a sweet treat, she helped Sky set the picnic table. She and her father helped clear the dishes when the meal ended. The feast left them pleasantly sated and, as the sun began to set, the new autumn air turned bitingly cool. The party moved inside, where the threesome sat side by side on the living room sofa, watching an Andy Griffith rerun in black-and-white on Sky's TV. Face, sprawled on the floor at their feet, sat up now and again to receive a pat from Sally or

Chet. When the program ended, they moved into the kitchen, and Sky made sundaes for dessert. It was dark when she packed up another bag of chocolate chip cookies for Sally. "You still have enough to feed an army," Chet observed as she closed the door on the half-dozen still full containers lining the pantry shelves. "Next time you can't sleep, give me a call. I'll talk you through it."

"Choco-non?" she teased.

"Something like that," he said, laughing. He slipped his arm around her waist and took Sally's hand. He looked from the girl to the woman and grinned. "I could spend the rest of my life like this, right here between my two best girls."

Sally tugged his arm. "C'mon, Daddy. I want to see Tootsie before bedtime."

Chet let himself be led into the foyer, but refused to let Sky out of his grasp. In the opened doorway, he pulled her closer still and lightly brushed his mustache across her lips. "Sleep tight," he sighed. "Don't let the chocolate chips bite."

Side by side, Face and Sky watched until the red glow of his tail lights was no longer visible. "Off he goes, into the wild black yonder," she sighed. And Face barked her agreement.

❧

She'd planned to leave with the cubs for Beartooth at dark. But, exhausted, Sky decided to wait until tomorrow night instead; after a good night's sleep and a long, restful day, she'd be far better prepared to tackle the wilderness, anyway.

Two hours later, snuggled under Gran's afghan, thinking of Chet and Sally's visit blotted the threatening note and calls from her mind, and she lounged languidly on the living room sofa. The pianist's rendition of Chopin's *Prelude in C Minor* tinkled from the stereo speakers, and the latest issue of *Health* magazine sat in her lap. "Don't ever fall in love," she said, petting the dog beside her. "It'll turn you into a featherbrained twit who can't get through one paragraph without thinking of—"

Face sat up and cocked her head toward the front door.

Tires crunched up the gravel driveway. *Slam* went a car door. A second later, footsteps thumped across the porch, followed by three hard knocks. "Some watchdog you are," she said to the Irish setter as she scurried into the foyer. "Where's your ferocious bark when I need it?"

The dog didn't seem the least bit frightened.

"Well, I'm scared enough for the both of us," she whispered. It never dawned on her that Face's reaction meant friend, not foe, stood on the other side of the front door.

Sky's heart lurched with fear and the blood in her veins felt icy cold. She headed for the foyer, turning out lights as she went, and grabbed Wade's police flashlight from its new storage spot on the table beside the door. Resting it on one shoulder like a rifle, she tiptoed to the door.

The moment she recognized the massive silhouette centered in the door's etched glass window, Sky immediately relaxed. Her life's motto pinged softly in the back of her mind, but Sky ignored it, and controlled the urge to throw open the door and leap into his arms.

"Sky…it's me."

"Why are you whispering?" she whispered back, grinning when she opened the door.

Chet stared at her as Face, tail wagging, whimpered for his attention. Distractedly, he patted her head, his eyes never leaving Sky. "I just stopped by to make sure you were all right."

"Wouldn't it have been easier to phone?"

"You have a lovely telephone voice," he said, stepping into the foyer and closing the door quietly behind him, "but it pales in comparison to the in-person voice." He took the flashlight from her hand and placed it on the foyer table. "Planning to bop me with that, were you?"

She glanced at it, then looked back at him. "No. It's just…. I thought…. I was afraid you were…."

The dark brows above his gray eyes furrowed. "So. Miss Brave and Able does have fears," he said, interrupting her stammering. Without another word, he picked her up, carried her into the living room, and deposited her gently on the couch. The house was totally dark, except for the lamp that glowed on the table beside the couch.

Chet sat beside her. "The real reason I'm here," he began, "is to tell you that…. Is to say I'm…." He cleared his throat. "I, uh, I'd like to know if you'd…."

His sigh, long and loud, seemed to hang in the air for several seconds. Sky wished she knew what to say or do to relieve his obvious discomfort.

"It's been a long time," he continued at last, "since I've felt like this," he murmured, staring at his hands, folded in his lap. "About a woman, I mean…."

If she had one measly ounce of courage, she'd have admitted she'd *never* felt this way about a man.

He turned a little to face her and draped an arm over her shoulders. "So I was wondering…."

She watched him intently, patiently, and waited.

"I was wondering if…if you'd consider…."

He stared across the room, toward the wide picture window, and blew a stream of air between his teeth. "I prayed about this all the way over here," he admitted, shaking his head. Then, meeting her eyes, he grinned. "Been prayin' about this for days, if you want to know the truth. You'd think all that conversin' with God would make things easier, wouldn't you?"

Sky didn't speak, didn't even nod. Was he about to propose?

"Guess the best way to do this is just to spit it out." He

took another gulp of air, then faced her again. "Would you be my girl, Sky?"

Blinking, she repeated the question in her mind. Repeated it again. The tremor in his voice, the worry lines on his brow, the serious way his eyes held hers, inspired slow laughter to bubble from her.

"What's so funny?" he wanted to know, his frown intensifying.

"I thought …," she began, giggling harder, "it sounded like …well, like you were revving up to propose."

Chet's brows rose high on his forehead. He chuckled. "I guess it did start off sounding that way, didn't it?" he admitted, squeezing her shoulder.

Laughing, and engrossed in the new closeness of their relationship, Sky and Chet didn't notice the quiet crunch of gravel in the driveway, and they ignored Face's whimpering. They didn't hear the footsteps that thudded across the yard as the shadowy figure darted from behind a giant spruce to crouch beside Chet's truck.

The dark figure had hidden the beat-up old Jeep deep in the pines on the other side of the highway, more than a mile away, but even the jog down her long, winding driveway had done little to warm him from autumn's cold night air. For weeks, he'd been showing up this way, always at a different time, hoping to catch a glimpse of her with the cubs. He'd grown accustomed to the irregular stream of visitors who showed up at the clinic while the sky was bright. But, so far during his surveillance, no one had come to Magic Mountain at this hour.

He'd heard the motor long before he saw the vehicle and he hid behind a fat tree trunk. The moment it passed by, he recognized it as Chet's truck, and he wondered what had brought the rancher all the way out here so late at night.

eleven

Chet had been gone for less than a minute when the grandfather clock chimed twelve times. Sky stood alone in the foyer, hugging herself and humming happily.

Scuffling and shouts interrupted her song and then suddenly Chet was on the porch again, hollering for her to call the sheriff. Sky opened the door, and gaped in fear. When he'd left, warmth glowed in his eyes. Now, they blazed with violent rage. At the end of one beefy arm, he held a very rumpled, very terrified Joe Peebles by the scruff of the neck. "I was almost at the end of the drive when I saw him slinking around in the trees," Chet thundered.

"I jus' w-w-wanted to see fer myself," Joe stammered. "I ain't never s-s-seen no w-w-wolf cubs before."

As long as she'd known him, Martha's lanky middle-aged son had never been anything but gentle and kind, and he cowered under Chet's angry glare. "You're hurting him, Chet. Let him go!"

Chet turned his glowering gaze on Sky. "Let him go! Are you crazy? I find him skulking around in the middle of the night, and you tell me to let him go?"

Sky pried Chet's fingers from Joe's shirt collar and straightened the thin man's eyeglasses. "What are you doing out here at this time of night?"

Dumbly, Joe shrugged and shook his head. "I j-j-just wanted to see the w-w-wolves."

"Have you been calling here and writing notes?" Chet demanded.

The anger in his voice was enough to make Joe take a step back. "Ma don't let me use the phone. On account of the time I dialed Hawaii by m-m-mistake." He looked at Sky. "'Member?"

She smiled gently and patted his hand. "Yes. I remember."

"Come on, Sky," Chet grumbled, rubbing his eyes. "Are you going to call the sheriff, or do I have to do it?"

Sky leveled an impatient look at Chet. "Will you please calm down and just think about this for a minute? You know Joe as well, even better, than I do. You've been doing business at The Grainery for years. Have you ever known him to be anything but honest?"

The fury in his eyes dimmed slightly. "Well, no. But...."

"I'd know that voice on the telephone anywhere. It wasn't Joe's. Besides," she added, looking back at her slow blinking friend, "He doesn't write notes. He prints. Isn't that right, Joe?"

Joe nodded so quickly, he momentarily lost his balance. "'Cause this hand don't w-w-work too good," he said, flexing the withered appendage.

She sent Chet an I-told-you-so look that diffused his remaining wrath. He lifted his chin defiantly and crossed his arms over his chest. "That doesn't explain what he's doing here at midnight."

Blushing, Joe stared at the toes of his loosely tied sneakers. "Some of the cowboys in Ma's store s-s-said Sky had wolf cubs on Magic Mountain." He looked at Chet. "I ain't never seen baby w-w-wolves. Not up close, anyways. So I borrowed Ma's Jeep." He patted his pocket, where the keys jangled quietly. "Those cubs s-s-sure are cute. Are they as soft as they l-l-look, Sky?"

Chet stepped up beside Sky and slid his arm protectively

around her waist. "Did you actually see any wolves around here, Joe?"

When he nodded, his glasses slid down his nose. "Uh-huh. An' I—h-heard 'em, too. They sure sound s-s-scary when they howl, don't they?"

Sky and Chet exchanged what-are-we-gonna-do-now? glances. "But why so late at night, Joe?" Chet pressed.

Joe's flush deepened and he grinned crookedly. "Baby animals need to eat every two hours. You taught me that, Sky. You taught me," he said, excitement raising his voice in pitch and volume. "I saw you go down by the shed at ten o'clock. I saw with my bin-no-noculars. You put that big light on, and I-I-I could see real good. I w-w-was gonna wait two more hours so I could s-s-see 'em again." Joe held up his arm and showed Sky his wristwatch. Then, staring at the toes of his sneakers again, he added quietly, "Only...only I f-f-fell asleep."

His hazel eyes, magnified several times by the farsighted lenses of his eyeglasses, focused on Chet. "That's w-w-why I was in the w-w-woods when your t-t-truck woke me up."

Snickering, Joe hid behind his gnarled hand. "I know what you guys were doin'. You guys were kissin' an stuff, like in the movies, weren't ya?"

Wry amusement had crinkled the corners of Chet's eyes when Sky glanced up at him. Sky sighed, relieved that this particular bomb, at least, had been diffused. "I don't know about anybody else," she said, "but I'm thirsty. How about a cup of tea?"

"Sure," Joe said, holding up three fingers. "I like three sugars."

Chet squeezed her hand. "I'd better head on out. Are you sure you're gonna be okay?"

She returned the squeeze. "I'll be fine." To Joe, she said,

"The teapot is on the counter. Would you mind filling it with water for me and putting it on the stove to boil?"

Joe shuffled toward the kitchen. "Sure, Sky. Sure."

Once Joe was out of earshot, Chet took her in his arms. "I'll call you first thing in the morning."

She felt so warm and safe there that Sky forgot, for a moment, about the cubs, the threatening notes, and the scary phone calls. "It *is* first thing in the morning."

"Then I'll call at some hour that rational people consider to be morning." He kissed her, then added, "Because I'm certainly not rational. Not after tonight." He gave her a long, meaningful look. "Don't stay up too long. It's been quite a day."

A monumental, momentous, unforgettable day, she thought, smiling. The sight of his hand on the doorknob made her heart ache. She didn't want him to leave. "I wish you could stay," she admitted, her voice softly pleading.

"So do I."

The tenderness on his face felt almost as comforting as one of his big bear hugs and it kept her warm inside for a long while after he left.

੨੪

Chet had been gone nearly half an hour when Sky refilled Joe's teacup. She'd told him the whole story by then. He may have been slow mentally, but he wasn't stupid.

"I don't like this," he said, his bushy brows knitted in a concerned pout. "Nope. Don't like this one bit. That bad guy wants those cubs real bad. He could maybe try to hurt you to get them, Sky."

She noticed that he hadn't stammered once during his warning. Suddenly, Joe's fist crashed onto the table. "I have a great idea!" he shouted. "Why don't we put 'em in my secret place! Nobody knows 'bout my secret place!" Joe jumped up and ran around and around the table, looking like a giant flamingo as his long arms flapped. Face, who'd been half asleep at Sky's feet, yipped with glee as she joined his circular romp.

The clock said 3:55; she'd been up nearly twenty-four hours. Sky didn't know what caused it, Joe's silly display of excitement or lack of sleep, but she laughed long and hard, and it took a full minute to get control of herself. Wiping tears of laughter from her cheeks, she patted the seat of Joe's chair. "Sit down and tell me about your secret place, Joe. Is it far away? In town, maybe?"

Joe bounced up and down in the chair, hardly able to contain himself. "No, no; not in town. In the foothills. Beartooth Plateau. It's a cave, see. I found it after Pa died. I used to go there when I missed him. It helped me stop being sad." Joe pushed his glasses higher on his narrow nose. "Now I go there when I'm tired of workin' in the store."

Sky remembered Martha's complaint: "Guess you'll have to load your own skid; Joe's missin' again." And when he returned, Joe stubbornly refused to discuss his absences. But the fact that he'd kept his place under wraps for nearly twenty years told Sky that Joe could be trusted with her secret.

As he began listing the features of the place, his usually-drowsy, liquid eyes glowed with life and intelligence. "It's very big. And the cubs couldn't get wet in there. Some caves leak, you know. I keep lanterns and flashlights and a sleeping bag up there. Sometimes I cook, too." Joe nodded, explaining that he'd built a stove from rocks and an oven rack he'd bought at the junk yard for a nickel. "It never gets smoky," he continued, his forehead furrowing as he scratched his head. "I don't know why, but it never gets smoky."

Moving the cubs to Joe's cave might just solve a few of her problems, at that. It would place them smack dab in the middle of the very place where she'd eventually release them. They could slowly grow accustomed to the sounds and scents that would be their home. She could teach them to hunt there.

The only problem Sky could see was that involving Joe would put him in the very same danger she'd been in since rescuing the cubs.

twelve

The kitchen clock said 10:15. Sky told Chet as he left that she'd stop by before lunchtime to check on Tootsie. If she hurried, she could shower and change before heading out to Four Aces. *The cubs are finally safe, and so are you. What more could you ask for?* Only one thing came to mind: Wade. He'd have been proud of what she'd accomplished in her twenty-seven years.

Driving to Four Aces, Sky saw the rocky cliffs and the broad fields through new eyes. She'd always cherished the vast beauty of Montana's landscape but because it had been Wade's birthplace, bits and pieces of his life seemed to echo from the hills and valleys: The big rock where he'd taught her to tie her shoes; the giant pine where he'd carved her name; the mountain peak that he'd said was her very own castle in the sky. Suddenly, memories that once caused pain now brought pleasure. She felt as though her smile began deep in her soul and radiated outward and, when she parked her truck outside Chet's barn, Dale greeted her, saying, "Looks like you just swallowed a gallon of happy juice. Love sure does agree with you."

She sent her friend a slice of that whole-body smile she'd been feeling. She dismissed her life's motto and prayed that this time, things would be different.

Sky was on her hands and knees, examining Tootsie's leg, when Chet appeared out of nowhere. "How's our patient, Doc?"

She hadn't thought it possible for her spirits to soar any

higher...until she heard the sound of his voice. "No infec-
tion," she announced, replacing the bandage. "But I'm going
to give her another dose of antibiotic, just in case."

His arms rested atop the stall's gate as he watched Sky
administer the medication. He was still watching as she
packed up her supplies. "How do you feel about pot roast?"

Looking into his eyes made her feel helpless and small,
like she'd been swallowed up by a deep gray ocean. Sky's
heart swelled with emotion. "You have a talent for asking
left field questions," she said, getting to her feet. "Pot roast,
huh? Well, Gran made a roast once that nearly choked me,
but I'm not the kind of woman who'd judge 'em all by the
bad behavior of one."

He leaned his chin on the back of his hand and grinned.
"We eat at seven, and Stella likes us to dress for dinner."

Stella. Hard-nosed, tight-lipped, thick-skinned Stella. The
mere mention of her name cooled the space between them.
As kids, Dale and Sky had put Stella in the same fear-induc-
ing category as Dorothy's wicked witch. Bud may have done
all the barking at Four Aces, but everybody in Mountain Gate
knew it was Stella who had the bite. Sky had never seen her
hug Ella; Bud, either, for that matter. In fact, she couldn't
remember hearing her utter a kind word to human or animal.
Sky couldn't imagine eating a peaceful meal at the same table
with the Ice Lady...and her bounty-hunting spouse.

Sky grimaced. "I don't know, Chet. I didn't exactly win
any Brownie points with Stella yesterday; maybe you could
just drive over to my place after sup—"

He walked over and affectionately tucked her hair behind
her ears. "Nonsense. I'll pick you up at six-thirty." That
said, he took her medical bag from her hands and put it on the
floor beside them, then drew her into a loose embrace.

Being in his arms felt so right and so good that Sky wondered why she'd fought it at first. Looking up into his hand-some face, she smiled. She'd never noticed the freckles that flecked across the bridge of his nose and she let her fingertips linger there, as if counting them, one by one. And as the thick soft mustache above his upper lip swept across her cheeks, she discovered it wasn't just black, but mahogany and cinnamon and gold, too, just like the luxurious hair on his head. He had the high-angled cheeks of a Cheyenne and a strong Irish nose, and her hands molded to his sun-kissed skin the way a sculptress handles firm fresh clay.

Sky knew she'd never tire of looking at him, but closed her eyes to test her memory of that noble face. She inhaled deeply, wanting scent and sight to create a singular image when she slept alone that night.

"You smell like a cowboy," he said, grinning. "A woman after my own heart."

ঽৰ

The moment she opened the front door, Sky knew she'd cho-sen her outfit wisely, for his eyes widened and he uttered a low growl of approval. Her hair fell in soft waves and touched the shoulders of her long-sleeved black dress. The knit fab-ric clung subtly, then flowed free and loose above her knees.

At five feet, nine inches tall, Sky usually wore flats or pumps so she wouldn't tower over male dinner companions. But even in two-inch-high heels, she felt petite beside Chet.

"Mmm, mmm, mmm," he said, nodding approvingly, "you look good enough to eat."

You will not blush, you will not blush! she insisted. He seemed to favor starched white shirts, which was fine with Sky, since she loved the way they accented his tanned com-plexion. His gray sportscoat matched his eyes and the legs of his navy trousers had such sharp creases that Sky feared they might draw blood if she stood too near.

"Don't want to mess your makeup," he whispered, "but I just gotta have a predinner treat." After one savory kiss, he whisked her away in the silver Porsche.

Stella sat stiffly in her teal wingback chair as Chet made introductions. "She was a childhood friend of Ella's, you know."

At the mention of his daughter's name, Bud's dark eyes brightened. "Yeah, Sky here spent many a summer day out on the veranda, didn't you, Sky?"

Sky hoped her lips would stop quivering. She smiled. During the ride to Four Aces, she'd promised herself there'd be no talk of wolves or bounties. She'd prepared herself for the Ice Lady's reception and for Bud's grumpy attitude. But Sky hadn't figured on anybody mentioning Ella. Her heart ached. "Some of my fondest childhood memories were made right here in this room."

Stella harumphed and adjusted the hem of her silk dress. "You get more flies with honey," she could hear Wade saying. She ignored Stella's attitude and grinned. "You look lovely in that shade of blue, Mrs. Houghton. It brings out the color of your eyes."

Blinking, the old woman touched a hand to her well-coiffed, cotton-white hair. "Yes. Well. Thank you." She looked at Bud. "Is it seven yet?"

He held a gold watch at the end of its sparkling, thick-linked chain. It made a quiet *click* as he popped open the lid. "Five minutes of," he said, and snapped it shut.

Sally dashed into the room and wrapped Sky's knees in a hug. "Dr. Allen! I'm so glad you're here!"

Minutes later, in the dining room, Stella dictated the seating arrangement so that Sky sat alone facing Chet. Sally sat to his right, and Stella and Bud took their places at opposite ends of the long mahogany table. China, crystal, and silver flatware gleamed atop a hand embroidered white-on-white tablecloth, and a second chandelier, smaller than the one in the huge foyer, rained aurora borealis-like light down upon them.

Chung grasped Stella's water goblet in a white-gloved hand. "Missy rike wa-tah?" he asked as he filled her glass. After putting it back at the two o'clock position beside her plate, he flapped her crisp white napkin and placed it neatly in her lap. Chung repeated the process until everyone had been watered and napkined. "Be back in jiffy," he said, then disappeared into the kitchen. He returned a moment later, pushing a food-laden brass cart. "Got rotsa good stuff here. You gonna eat prenty, okay?"

"Shall we say grace?" Stella interrupted. "Sally, please fold your hands. Bud, put down that glass. Chester," she said, "since she's your guest, will you do the honors?" Stella said "guest" as though Sky had landed on the roof in a pink flying saucer and, since the question was more an order than a request, Sky marveled that Chet didn't even seem to notice Stella's haughty attitude. Sky bowed her head and resisted the temptation to peek up at Chet as he prayed:

"Lord, bless this food and those who prepared it, and bless us who sit together at this table. We thank You for this glorious bounty, for good health, and happiness. In the name of the Father, and of the Son, and of the Holy Ghost…whoever eats the fastest gets to eat the most." When Chet lifted his head, he winked mischievously and ground his palms together. "Pass the spuds, Doc."

Stella gasped and Sally giggled and Bud rolled his eyes, as if Chet's shenanigans were a daily affair.

It was thanks to his constant light-hearted banter that the dinner conversation remained light and enjoyable. By the time Chung handed out the last plate of homemade apple pie, even Stella wore a relaxed smile on her face.

As he drove Sky back to Magic Mountain, Chet asked, "Where'd you Allens get a name like 'Magic Mountain,' anyway?" as his headlights illuminated the sign at the end of her driveway. "Sounds like an amusement park ride."

Sky laughed. The similarity had never even occurred to her before, but he definitely had a point. "Leave it to you to find the ridiculous in the sublime," she said, laughing. "Unfortunately, there's no poetic story to explain the name. Gramps always said the view of Granite Peak was magical. After he said it a couple thousand times, the name just kind of stuck."

He was still chuckling as they stepped into her foyer. Stella, lima beans and peas, and her homestead's name were the furthest things from her mind when Chet wrapped her in a hug and kissed her. "I've been dying to do that all night." Face insisted on some attention, too, and Chet obligingly doled it out. "Did I tell you that I fell asleep last night thanking God that you said you'd be my girl?"

Blushing, she stepped out of his hug. "Oh, Chet. I've never been the answer to a prayer before. I sure hope I'm worthy—"

The answering machine on the desk in the living room blinked, telling Sky she had one call. "Let me make sure nobody has a sick cow or anything," she said, grinning. Standing beside her, he hugged her as she depressed the message button.

"Just one more day, and you're gonna find out that we're not foolin'," said the raucous, gritty voice. "Get rid of those cubs, or you'll be sorry."

thirteen

Chet gently pushed Sky aside and pressed the rewind button. After he'd listened to the message a second time, he paced between the couch and the coffee table. "He said he wasn't fooling. He's called before?"

He was angrier than she'd ever seen him and Sky knew from experience how single-minded he could be when in this mood. She braced herself for the storm that would surely follow.

"How many times?" he demanded, ripping off his tie and flinging it onto the couch. "And just exactly how long were you planning to hide them from me?"

Sky picked up his rumpled tie and draped it neatly over the arm of the couch. "I never saw a need to involve you in my personal problems," she said, smoothing the navy silk.

He sat on the edge of the desk and crossed his arms over his chest. The grandfather clock in the foyer chimed ten times as he stared at her. When the last hollow note stopped echoing, he shook his head. "*Your* personal problems," he repeated, his voice a raspy whisper. "That hurts, Sky. I thought …." But he never finished his sentence. Instead, he pressed his fingertips into his eyes.

Sky inhaled deeply and fiddled with her watchband, then removed her earrings and put them on the end table. This whole wolf thing had become a maddening, frustrating mess. What started out as her simple attempt to right one wrong had gone all wayward and cockeyed, getting more dangerous and more frightening by the minute. Sky ran her hands through her hair and held them there, uncertain what to do or say to make him understand that the responsibility for the cubs was hers alone; that she'd decided on the day she sequestered them in the shelter that no one else would be involved...no one else should be involved...or endangered...as a result of her decision.

"I wish I could make you understand," she said, her voice quaking with emotion. "Sally has already lost one parent. I won't make you a part of anything that might cost her another."

He looked up so suddenly that a lock of dark hair fell over one eye. The fierce scowl on his face softened. In two long strides, he was holding her close. "You're forgetting that I'm part Cheyenne," he whispered into her hair. "I have special powers that protect me from evil, you know," he teased. Tenderly, Chet kissed her forehead. "But I must admit, I'm very touched that you're worried about me."

When she met his eyes and saw the familiar teasing glint sparkling there, Sky's heart lurched.

"I'm stronger than I look," he said, his grin slanting the thick dark mustache. "Why, just this afternoon, I lifted a veterinarian into the air with my bare hands."

From the corner of her eye, she saw the red flash of the answering machine, a steady reminder that the longer Chet stayed with her, the more likely he was to be hurt because of her cubs.

Tears filled her eyes and she swiped angrily at them. *Be strong*, she told herself, *and do the right thing!* "I think you'd better leave."

Chet's brows rose in silent confusion. "You don't mean that." His smile faded and the lusty light in his eyes dimmed.

Tearing herself from the wonderful warmth of his arms was one of the hardest things she'd ever done. She turned her back on him. "Yes. I do." Hugging herself, she bit her lower lip to keep from crying.

"You're not fooling me. You have every right to be afraid. In fact, I'm glad you're afraid. It tells me you've finally come to your senses and have realized how serious this wolf situation is."

He hadn't moved. Sky guessed the distance between them to be less than a yard, though at that moment, it seemed more like a mile.

"Sky," he said softly, "c'mere. Please?"

She wanted to run to him and throw herself into his arms and hold on for dear life. Wanted it more than anything. But Sky stood her ground. She could protect him now only by rejecting him.

"I'm awfully tired." She didn't want him to see her tears, so Sky continued to stand with her back to him. "I'd really appreciate it if you'd just go now."

Tick, tick, tick said Gran's clock, the only sound in the room.

Face padded up to Sky and sat in front of her, those coppery eyes filled with concern and compassion at her mistress' discomfort. When the dog whimpered, Sky stooped to hug her. "Everything's okay, girl. Stop your worrying, all right?"

Face glanced at Chet, then sauntered over to him. "Don't believe a word she says," he told the dog. "She's got herself in so deep, she can't see her way out."

Face barked and whined, then lay on the floor between them, looking helplessly from Chet to her mistress and back again.

Tick, tick, tick....

Suddenly, he was behind her, turning her around, wrapping her in those big, strong, comforting arms. "Beat me with a stick," he sighed. "Jab a needle in my eye. Burn me with a hot poker. Shoot me in my good leg, even. Just don't send me away, Sky. Please...."

It was the last thing on earth she wanted to do. But like it or not, it was the very thing she had to do.

"We can beat this thing…together."

Together…. The word said two as one and happily ever after and till death us do part. If only it could be.

Tick, tick, tick….

Sky closed her eyes and pictured Sally, wide eyed and innocent and very much dependent on her daddy.

"I'll talk to the sheriff. I'll have Dale camp out here with a loaded shotgun," he said. "We'll call out the National Guard if we have to."

"In just a few months, I'll be able to let the cubs go, and this whole thing will be over." *Wait for me,* she implored silently. She lifted her chin defiantly, her left brow arching slightly—a trick she'd learned from an expert conversation manipulator—and added, "Until then, I can't see you." She'd put extra emphasis on the "until" part of her demand and prayed he'd heard and understood exactly what it meant.

With that, she stepped into the foyer and opened the front door. Standing there, one hand on the gleaming brass handle and one on her hip, Sky stared at him, willing him through the door and out of her life…for now, anyway. Her breaths came in short, shallow gasps and her heart raced, but she pressed her lips tightly together to give the illusion, at least, of determination and strength.

His bulk filled the living room doorway. He'd gotten that far, but couldn't seem to take those final steps through the foyer and out of her house. She recognized that pained look in his eyes. It was the same expression she'd seen that night on her porch, when he'd told her about losing Ella. Her heart ached at having been responsible for putting more pain in his life.

"Sky, this isn't necessary, I'm telling you."

She took a deep breath. "It's absolutely necessary." And with a wave of her hand, she invited him to walk through the door.

"Fine," he snapped, nodding furiously. "If that's the way you want it.… Two can play this game."

The moment he was on the porch, Sky slammed the door behind him and locked it. Leaning against the smooth cool wood, she listened as he revved the Porsche's engine, continued to listen as it spit gravel when he tore down the driveway in his pain and fury, and listened to the silence that screamed "He's gone!"

Several times that night, she woke with a start, thinking she heard his car, his voice, his footsteps on the porch. In those few restless hours when she did manage to doze, she dreamed of him. Of his laughing gray eyes and his wide winning smile. When she woke for good at four-thirty, she dismally admitted she may very well have saved him…only to lose him forever.

fourteen

"What are you doing here?" Sky had been out all morning, visiting Joe and the cubs, making house calls, and running errands. It wasn't hard to sound tired and cold, hard and unfeeling. Sky tried to look angry and put out as she walked toward the porch, her backpack slung over one shoulder. "I thought I made myself clear last night."

"You did a lot of talking," Chet drawled, chewing the tip of a toothpick. "I don't know if I'd say you were clear."

Dark circles beneath his beautiful eyes told her he hadn't slept much, either. She wanted to kiss each worry line from his brow. Instead, she glanced at her watch. "I've been up since dawn, and I still have a very full day ahead of me," she said stiffly. "Whatever brought you here...." She reminded herself that he'd never said he loved her. Those words would have made all the difference in the world. "Make it quick."

Face wagged her tail and insisted on a pat. Obligingly, Chet gave it, then plopped down in Gran's chair once more. "Have a seat, Sky."

She dropped the backpack onto the porch floor and sat in Gramps' rocker. "Pull up a chair. Make yourself at home. Have a seat, Sky," she mocked.

Chet's eyes narrowed dangerously. "Why do you always make a joke when things scare you?"

Sky sat up straighter. "You don't scare me."

He took a deep, exasperated breath. "I feel like I'm talking to Sally," he said to the porch ceiling. "Well, all right," he added, meeting her eyes, "if you insist on behaving like a spoiled brat, that's the way I'll deal with you." Chet leaned forward and balanced his elbows on his knees, that left brow high on his forehead. "I'm not going to say this more than once, so pay attention: I care what happens to you, though for the life of me I don't know why…what with all your female mind-changing antics…and I want to help pull you out of this hole you've dug yourself into, so we can begin living some kind of normal existence around—"

She held up a hand to silence him. "*If* I'm in any hole," she began slowly, "I'm very comfortable in it alone, thank you."

"So you said last night. 'I'm kicking you out for your own good until the cubs are gone,'" he paraphrased, his voice thick with sarcasm. Wagging his forefinger inches from her nose, he added, "I just thought it fair to warn you: I'm not that easy to dismiss."

He was leaning on the back of Gran's chair, shaking his head. He moved around to the front of the chair and stood, feet firmly planted a shoulder's width apart, facing her. "Those wolves of yours are tearing more than us apart. They're tearing the whole town apart. If I had the key to your grandfather's shelter, I'd shoot the little beasts myself and put an end to this whole sorry mess, once and for all!"

Fury flowed from his eyes like molten steel and she believed he meant it…at least at that moment. "And that," she said, brewing a little fury of her own, "is precisely why I asked you to stay away from me. You see me as a helpless female, desperately in need of the protection of a big strong male. Well, I'm not helpless, and I certainly don't need your protection!"

Chet pursed his lips, then grinned crookedly.

Oooh, how she loved that grin. She stood there in silence, hands clenched into fists at her sides, trembling with rage.

Two steps—that's all it would take—and she'd be in his arms, welcoming the kisses that would make her forget cubs and notes and calls. Just two steps. Sadly, she admitted it may as well have been a hundred miles.

He seized her eyes in a hot gaze and refused to let go, daring her to deny her true feelings. "You sure are gorgeous when you're angry. For two cents, I'd kiss you, right where you stand."

Sky didn't know what possessed her to do it, but she reached into her pocket, withdrew two pennies, and tossed them at his feet.

He stared at the coins for a moment, then looked up at her. Chet took a step. Sky took a step. And the hundred-mile gap between them closed. "You make me crazy," he said, hugging her tightly. "Don't ever do that again; don't ever say you don't want me around."

You're a weak, pathetic pushover, she told herself, closing her eyes as he dotted sweet kisses across the bridge of her nose, on her cheeks and chin. "I wanted you to stay away until...."

No man had ever looked at her that way before, and Sky's heart soared. If it wasn't love sparkling in his eyes, she'd settle for whatever it was. She'd seen a leaf float into a whirlpool once. Watched it whirl round and round, down, down, until it disappeared into the deep, fast rushing river. In his arms, Sky felt a lot like that helpless little leaf.

When his lips touched hers, Sky tried to say that she loved him. Somehow, she couldn't get the words out. She'd just have to show him, instead, with a lifetime of devotion and care.

"I'm crazy about you," he said.

He'd said "crazy." She heard "love."

The phone rang and rang. She couldn't ignore it, yet she

had no desire to go inside to answer it. She didn't want the happy moment to end.

He seemed able to read her mind, and led her by the hand into the living room, where he picked up the receiver and placed it gently beside her ear. "I'm going to get us some lemonade," he whispered, pointing toward the kitchen door.

She nodded and smiled, happier than she'd been in a long, long time. "Hello?" She hoped whoever was on the other end wouldn't hear the pleasant contentedness in her voice.

"It's Saturday."

Instantly, the tranquility of the moment was whipped away and now she felt like a leaf in a hurricane. "I'm sorry," she said, sitting on the arm of the couch. "I'm afraid I didn't hear you."

"I said it's Saturday. You only have 'til Sunday to get rid of the cubs. That doesn't leave you much time."

"But I don't have any cubs," she said truthfully, thankful he'd given her a chance to speak this time.

"You have them. Don't deny it."

"I have a dog. An Irish setter. But there are no wolves here."

"You're a terrible liar, Doc. You have two gray wolves. Four months old, give or take a week. A male and a female; the male's the bigger. You write stuff about them in a blue and maroon journal. You were feeding them every two hours at first; then every four. Then a morning and an evening meal. They're down to every other day now. And just a few days ago, you brought two big brown teddy bears down into that hole in the ground where you've got 'em stashed." He paused, then snickered sickeningly. "Need more proof that I know what I know?"

She trembled with terror. His information was accurate, all right. "I don't know where you're getting your information, but there are no—"

"I'm getting my information right from the horse's mouth," he interrupted. "I'll call you in a couple of days and let you know what kind of deal we're gonna make."

Maybe, if she chose her words carefully, she could convince him that the cubs were gone. "But I took your advice. I already let them go. If you watch as carefully as you say, surely you remember that I left here day before yesterday with a big box in my truck. The wolves were in it. I took them to—"

"I don't cotton to liars, Doc. I'll be in touch," he said, his laughter grating like coarse sandpaper through the wires as he hung up.

Almost immediately, the phone rang again. Chet walked back into the room carrying two glasses of milk in one big hand and a stack of chocolate chips in the other. "Don't answer it," he said, winking playfully.

She hoped he wouldn't read the panic in her eyes. "I have to. It could be a patient."

"I forgot to tell ya earlier," the voice grated into her ear, "it won't do any good to keep that cowboy around all the time."

She thought her heart might leap straight out of her chest.

"Hey, what's the matter?" Chet asked, putting the milk and cookies on the coffee table. "You're pale as a ghost."

Suddenly, he was sitting beside her, pointing at the receiver. "That's *him*, isn't it?"

Sky nodded.

Chet pressed his ear against the receiver and listened.

"I had him in my sights while he was sittin' in that stiff-backed old chair on your porch a little while ago. Would have been a shame to bloody up that pretty blue shirt of his—"

"Gimme that phone!" Chet raged. But by the time he put it to his ear, the caller had left him holding a dead line.

"Did you hear that?" she demanded, looking at Chet. "Do you get it now? Do you see why I don't want you around here?"

He hugged her. "I see why you're scared. Anybody in your shoes would be. This guy is more than we can handle on our own. You have to call the sheriff. He'll know what to do." He paused. "I know that voice. Why do I know that voice?"

If he recognized it, too, it must mean the gunman knew them both. Suddenly, Sky felt completely exposed. She pulled Gran's afghan onto her lap and shook her head furiously. Chet had said "we" and "us" and "our." Just last night, she'd successfully removed him from the danger. Now, thanks to her weak will, he was right back in the line of fire.

She hugged the afghan to her. "You have to leave. And don't come back again. I couldn't live with myself if anything happened to you. I... I...." Tears choked her words. Embarrassed by her show of weakness, she hid her face in the afghan.

Again, he gathered her into a warm, protective embrace. "Shhh," he soothed. "Once the cops are involved, everything will be just—"

She leaped up from the couch. "If you really care about us, you'll stay away from here...from me. And you won't call the police, either, because that would only put the cubs in more danger. I can handle this, Chet, if you'll just go away and let me do what's—"

Winking, Chet clasped his hands behind his head. "Mmm-mmm-mmm. The only way this guy's gonna keep me away from you, pretty lady," he said, smiling, "is to shoot me, right here." He put his fingertip between his eyebrows.

Sky gasped and her eyes filled with fresh tears. "Don't say things like that!" She grabbed his hands and pulled him to his feet. "I'm not kidding, Chet. I want you out of here. And you can't come back. You understand why, don't you?"

He held her close. "Okay. Okay, I'll go, if that's what it'll take to calm you down." Grimacing, he added, "I can't stand to see you like this." He kissed her tenderly.

Sky refused to participate in the kiss. She concentrated instead on what he'd said earlier about the hole she'd dug herself into. It gave her an idea and, if she played it out smartly, she might just still be able to save the cubs, and Chet, and herself, too.

fifteen

He loosened the knot of his tie and waited for the secretary to refill his coffee cup. "That'll be all, Missy," he said, smiling condescendingly, his casual wave telling her what his words needn't have. Mike Rowen had been summoning and dismissing people for so long, it was second nature to him now. Rowen inhaled deeply from the cigarette between his fingers, then watched the gray-blue stream of smoke float from his lips toward the window wall. "So the good doctor is proving to be difficult, is she?" Crisp blue eyes bore into Bart, demanding an explanation.

Bart had been thumping and picking at the brass brads that held the supple red leather in place, but his hands froze when he noticed that Rowen's icy glare had zeroed in on his fingertips. Showing Mike Rowen your weakness would be tantamount to spreading honey all over yourself, then standing in front of a half-starved grizzly, Bart realized. He took a long slow sip of his coffee, buying time, trying to calm down. Trying to think up an excuse that would appease Rowen. "We're not dealing with some blond bimbo here, Mike," he said. "Sky Allen...she's smart. And she's got guts, too."

Rowen sat forward and leaned his elbows on the glass-topped mahogany desk. "Then you'll just have to be smarter."

His voice reminded Bart of every horror creature he'd ever seen in the movies: deep, grating, threatening. He clenched his teeth, making a thin line of his lips.

The green eyes darkened. "You'd be wise to keep that temper of yours in check, Bart, my boy. You're into me for half a million, don't forget."

How could he possibly forget, when the creep reminded him of his debt every step of the way? He sighed deeply, then ran a hand through his hair. He'd come to despise that smirking tanned face. Rowen hadn't earned his color with long hours of hard work, sweating in hot sunny fields, as he had. No. Rowen's golden glow was a rich man's tan, baked on in a tanning bed. *A gilded one probably,* Bart thought, grinning slightly, *with his initials etched on it.*

"You're finding something about our conversation amusing?" Rowen asked. "Maybe I'm making this too easy for you." He lit another cigarette and stared for a long time at the bright silver lighter. "No. I don't think so," he said. His words seemed to float on the smoke that encircled his head. "Obviously this job has been hard on you." Rowen winked and shook his head. "I'm noticing some gray streaks in those shining brown waves of late, my boy. You're beginning to look a little rough around the edges."

Rowen's perfect, practiced smile vanished, and Bart flinched. "I'm running out of time, Bart. Out of patience, too. Now, let's not kid ourselves…. Your ranch is a solid property. But it's not worth a tenth of what Sky Allen's is worth, and we both know why. We made a deal. Shook hands. In front of witnesses, need I remind you?"

Bart's hatred for the man intensified, but he swallowed hard to keep it hidden. When this sorry mess was over, he'd tell the fool to drop dead. Might even tell him with a doubled up fist. But until then, he had no choice but to be Rowen's whipping boy. Gambling and drinking had made him a target; he had no one to blame but himself for the mess he was in, and he knew it.

At that moment, Bart was glad his daddy had died last year. Because if he'd lived to see what a mess his youngest son had made of his life, he'd have died of a broken heart instead of a heart attack. Bart sipped his coffee. It was cold, bitter…like his life.

Rowen laughed softly, then walked around to the front of the big desk and perched on its corner. "I want you to listen to me, Bart, and listen good," he said, flapping a thick envelope. "I've got your family's ranch right here in the palm of my hand. You want to save it? You do things my way. And you do them quick, you got that?" The suave sophisticated voice had disappeared, replaced by an evil, grating sound.

Bart jumped up and, in one long stride, put himself directly in front of Rowen. One fist grabbed the wrist of Rowen's hand that held the deed to the Lazy L, and the other wadded Rowen's two-hundred-dollar silk tie. "You listen, you cocky, stuffed shirt. I don't like you. In fact, I've met mangy coyotes I like better." He shook the blond man for emphasis. Rowen's face was turning from tanned to beet red as Bart twisted the delicate fabric tighter against his throat.

"I'm gonna get you that Allen property because I said I would. Because I owe it to my daddy to protect that land. But until I do, you'd better show me a little respect." He looked down at his fist, and then, as though repulsed that he'd touched anyone so vile as Rowen, tossed the blond man backward on his desk.

Rowen smoothed the rumpled material. "And what if I don't?"

His "dare you" look infuriated Bart, whose blue eyes became slits. But then Bart grinned, laughed, opened his big arms wide. "I've got no wife. No kids. No family." He looked at the deed, still clasped tightly in Rowen's hand. "Maybe no home. You're lookin' at a man with nothin' to lose, *my boy.*"

"Get out," Rowen rasped, returning to the other side of his desk. "And don't you dare show your face around here again until you can give me something that says the Allen property is mine." His forefinger jabbed his appointment book as he added, "On the first of next month, the Lazy L will be mine, and I'll take great pleasure in kicking you off the place."

Bart's bulk filled the open doorway. His grin broadened as he pulled his hat lower on his forehead. He chuckled. "Not on your best day, Rowen. Not even on your best day."

But his smirk died even before he'd pushed the elevator's down button, because Bart knew that Rowen had him over a barrel. "Desperate men do desperate things," he'd said. "Find their weaknesses," his daddy had always said. And that's what he aimed to do.

He had a lot in common with Sky—just one of the many things he liked about her—and one of their common traits was that she had very little to lose, also.

Very little, maybe, but she did have one thing that meant something to her. And he was just desperate enough to use it.

&

Sky heard Face's familiar whimper on the other end of the line, but couldn't accept what he'd said. How could he have taken the dog captive? Placing her hand over the phone's mouthpiece, she cried, "Face! C'mere, girl!" If the dog had been within earshot, she'd have bounded onto Sky's bed in a whipstitch. But no happy feet came running. No friendly bark sounded at the end of the hall. No smiling doggy face met hers with adoring, damp kisses.

"You gotta be more careful, Doc," he advised. "This here's one purty little pup you've got. I bet I could get a hunnerd bucks for her in Livingston."

Again Face whimpered. "If you do anything to her, I'll ...."

"You'll what?" he growled. "*I've* got the upper hand now. And don't you forget it!"

Wade's voice echoed from somewhere deep in her memory. "Talking to a drunk is like talking to a wall," he would tell his daughter. As sheriff of Georgia's Fulton County, he'd arrested a dozen drunks a week. "You got to let 'em ramble 'til they're sober, *then* you let 'em have it."

Trying to keep a calm, even tone in her voice, Sky asked, "What do you want?"

He laughed a wicked little laugh. "So what's it gonna be, Doc? Do we have a deal?".

"I'm going to hang up and call the sheriff."

"And tell him what?"

He was right, of course. The recorded voice could have been anybody's, and anyone might have scribbled the note. By the time officials figured out who the madman was, he could have—

"Maybe you'd like a day or two to think it over," he said, interrupting her frenzied thoughts. And with that, he hung up.

The house seemed huge and empty without Face's constant companionship. Sky wandered from room to room, missing her quiet panting and the *click, click* of her toenails on the hardwood flooring. Again, her life's motto echoed in her head, taunting her. "If you'd followed the rules," it hinted, "you wouldn't be in this position now."

Chet had been right. She'd dug herself in so deeply that not even the sheriff could pull her out now.

She wanted to make the caller pay for stealing Face. For terrorizing her with phone calls and the terrifying note. For making her give up the only man she'd ever loved. But at this point, she was helpless to do anything. She couldn't call Dale; she certainly couldn't call Chet. If he'd take Face, there was no telling what he might be capable of doing…or to whom. She thought about that all through the long, sleepless night.

❧

Sky stood in the shower for a long time, letting the hot water pummel her weary body, hoping it would wash the tension and fear down the drain along with the sweet smelling suds. She made the decision as she towel dried her hair: She'd get the deed to Magic Mountain out of the safe deposit box at the bank, and see what, if anything, it said about that section of land along the highway.

As the hair dryer roared, Sky pictured the chunk of land. It was a dusty, rocky, barren tract. Its only redeeming quality was the beautiful spruce trees that grew close to the road. What did that awful man want with a piece of useless property?

And then Sky remembered reading in last week's paper that Rowen Construction had come to town, romancing farmers and ranchers in and around Mountain Gate. The huge development corporation built ski and beach resorts all over the country. They'd set their caps on Yellowstone territory this time. She realized that because her property ran along Route 212, it had become prime real estate, providing easy access to construction traffic now and tourist traffic later.

Once she understood the stakes, making the decision was easy. She'd get the deed to Magic Mountain out of her safe deposit box at the bank, and tell the maniac to do with it whatever he pleased. Because she was tired, so tired…of being in danger…of putting those she cared about in danger…and tired, too, of being afraid.

Mountain Gate had it all over Atlanta in most respects but, despite the way it rambled for miles in every direction, its small town atmosphere made keeping secrets and securing privacy sometimes difficult. In Atlanta, all she'd have to do to gain entry into the safe deposit box vault was show the clerk her key. In line at the bank, Sky wondered if Mrs. Warfield would ask the customary dozen questions when she requested access to her safe deposit box.

"Good morning, Sky," Mrs. Warfield said. "What can I do for you today?"

Sky showed the old woman her key. "I need to get into my safe deposit box."

Chet stepped into line behind her, but Sky was unaware of him.

"That might be a problem," Mrs. Warfield said. "They're laying new tiles back there, you see, and no one can walk on it yet."

Sky frowned. "Why didn't they do that after normal banking hours?"

She shrugged. "Nobody else seemed to mind."

"Well, I mind," Sky snapped. Then, in reaction to Mrs. Warfield's disdainful expression, she added, "I'll only be in there a minute or two. I promise to walk carefully...."

"I'll need to see what Mr. Harper says about that first. You wait right there," the old woman said before disappearing into the manager's office.

In the old woman's absence, Sky's nerves twitched. She hated banks and conducted business in them as seldom, and as quickly, as possible. Leaning on the shining marble counter, her head hurt and her stomach churned as she watched the camera on the opposite wall pan the bank's interior. The camera at First Atlanta Savings and Loan had made that same motorized noise on the day her father was gunned down. The vault behind the counter stood ajar; so had the vault in Georgia. Computers blinked. A telephone rang. The marble floors reflected the dim glow of overhead lights. And the unmistakable scent of metal money...all so reminiscent of the day her dad had been killed.

And ever since that horrible day in August, just before her seventeenth birthday, Sky couldn't enter a bank without connecting everything inside it with the smell of gunpowder and death. Wade had died a slow, painful death right before her eyes. Over and over she repeated Acts 2:24, "'Whom God hath raised up, having loosed the pains of death: because it was not possible that he should be holden of it,'" and took comfort in knowing the Lord would gently cradle her father throughout eternity as she'd gently cradled him on that fateful day.

Sky's stomach growled embarrassingly, reminding her she wasn't in Atlanta, at all, but Mountain Gate, Montana. She hadn't been eating properly, preferring instead to work through mealtimes as she had done in college and med school. In those days, hard work helped her forget the things that haunted her. She hoped it would help her forget what haunted her now. Like the man in the hills who seemed to watch her relentlessly. Joe, so innocent and dependent, alone in the cave with the wolf cubs. And the awful fight she had picked with Chet that day.

She'd wanted the man in the hills to see the anger, the pain, the resolution on Chet's face as he watched the dissolution of Sky and Chet's budding romance. So she said every angry, spiteful thing she could think to say. If she had to hurt him to save him, so be it, she'd decided.

She'd hurt him, all right. That much was evident in his clear gray eyes. Even knowing she'd done the right thing didn't make it easier. Her good deed came with a hefty price tag—long, lonely, sleepless nights.

Exhaustion and fear and frustration mounted as Sky waited for Mrs. Warfield to return from the bank's back room. What started as a quiet ringing in her ears became a loud underwater sound. A cold clammy sensation gripped her entire body as waves of dizziness rolled over her. Sky gripped the counter for support, hoping the sensation would pass quickly, but soon she was trembling all over. Her teeth chattered, yet her palms and brow and upper lip grew sticky with sweat. She was dizzy. So dizzy....

Sky had never fainted before. A silly grin spread across her face as she began to melt onto the hard polished floor. *There's a first time for everything* was her last conscious thought.

sixteen

Chet had been standing there, listening, trying to send Mrs. Warfield a telepathic message to let Sky into the vault. Because the sooner she got her way, the less time he'd have to spend looking at her...at those shiny auburn waves...at that stubborn lift of her chin...at the way she squared her shoulders....

At first, he'd thought it was his imagination when she began to sway at the counter. But when she started to slump toward the floor, Chet realized something was dreadfully wrong. When he took a step forward and held out his arms, Sky fell into them like a willing, weak child. He went to the floor with her, allowing his body to cushion hers.

Holding her there in his lap brought suppressed emotions to the surface. Since her tantrum in her front yard, he'd stubbornly refused to call her. He hadn't pulled into her driveway, though his pickup seemed determined to lurch in that direction every time he passed Magic Mountain on his way to or from town. He had told himself, over and over, that he had neither the time nor the patience for a woman whose emotions swung in such a wide arc. He'd spent time in the barn, more time in the fields, a lot more time with Sally.

But daisies were her favorite flowers and the wild ones that grew along the highway awakened vivid images of her. She had called Sally "little one," and now whenever the child said it to one of her stuffed animals, his heart ached with longing.

Seeing her this way unnerved him. She'd always been

strong, determined to do everything all by herself and all on her own. Holding her limp body against his chest filled him with an incredible fear. If he were smart, he'd hand her over to Mrs. Warfield who babbled nonsensically as she fanned Sky's face with an Open-a-New-Checking-Account brochure. Yes, hand her over and turn tail and run.

Because on the one hand, he was scared to death that the moment she opened her eyes, he'd blurt out how much he'd missed her. That life without her these past few weeks had been dull and dreary, like the dark days following Ella's death.

He stared into her pretty face, his big hands smoothing over her lightly freckled cheeks, wiping perspiration from her brow. He'd tried telling himself she was all wrong for him. That her stubborn streak and independent nature made her too high-strung for the likes of him. But then he'd remembered how quietly and calmly she'd soothed Sally the day Tootsie was injured, and he knew Sky was one of the most settled, stable people he'd ever met. He'd tried telling himself she'd been alone too long, that she'd developed habits and traits that would make life with her a nightmare. And then he'd re-called the ease with which she adjusted to new situations, despite all she'd lived through, and he knew that life with her would be a dream come true. He loved this woman like he'd never loved anyone. It hurt a little, admitting that, because for years he'd told himself he loved Ella with every fiber in his being. If Sky had never come into his life, he'd have gone right on missing Ella's happy chatter and sweet kisses, be-lieving that what they'd shared had been the epitome of love. He'd have gone the rest of his days, totally unaware that some-thing more existed, something deeper and more abiding, some-thing that fulfilled a burning, yearning, never-ending need.

The breath caught in his throat as her eyelids began to flut-ter. The moment her eyes met his, he had a profound desire to kiss her, for in that moment of unguarded confusion, he saw every ounce of love he felt for her coming right back at him, boring straight into his center. The only time he'd felt more vulnerable had been when the doctor had grabbed his hand in the hallway outside Ella's hospital room and said, "We're sorry, Chet...."

Sky eyes slowly glanced around at the rest of the worried faces that hovered above her. It seemed as natural as breathing to slip her arms around Chet's neck. "Hi," she whispered, a silly grin on her face. "What are you doing here?"

"You fainted," he explained, smiling and hugging her a little tighter.

"If it hadn't been for Chet," Mrs. Warfield said, "you'd probably have hit your head on this marble floor. Might have yourself a dandy concussion right about now."

Woozily, Sky interpreted the old woman's words. So he'd saved her again. Sky giggled, remembering that night on her porch when his strong presence had been the only thing between her and the hard porch floor.

That smell...those noises.

Suddenly, Sky remembered where she was. And why she'd come here. She tried to sit up. It surprised her when she couldn't and she emitted a tiny, frustrated sigh.

"What's your hurry?" he asked, holding her tighter.

"The deed...."

The worry furrow on his brow deepened. "What deed?"

Sky frowned. "Magic Mountain...."

"Why?"

"Because," she sighed, gripping his hand, "he has Face."

He'd wrapped his arms around her and now he pulled her closer. "Who has Face?" he asked, a ferocious, protective note in his voice.

Sky pushed his hands aside and sat up straight, then hid her

face behind her hands. It all came back to her in a rush—
what the man on the phone wanted, and why, and what he
might do if she didn't give it to him. *Can't tell Chet,* she
thought, her subconscious mind still sending choppy, frag-
mented messages to her conscious mind. *Have to do it alone.
Get the deed, for Face.*

Mr. Harper and Mrs. Warfield had wandered away and
stood near the counter, looking over at Sky, mumbling about
the bank's liability in case of a lawsuit. Chet continued to
hold onto her. His strength ebbed into her and, before long,
her breathing returned to normal and the dizzying waves
stopped crashing over her.

He'd been sitting cross-legged on the floor, cradling her in
his lap. Sky had managed to back away, but only partially.
And part of her didn't want to break the final connection.
"What have you been doing to yourself? You look horrible,"
he said.

Tucking in one corner of her mouth, she grinned. "Thanks.
You sure know how to turn a girl's head."

Chet ignored her. His stern glare told her he intended to
get answers to his questions. "When was the last time you
ate a decent meal?"

She shrugged. "I dunno. Yesterday, maybe?" She got onto
her knees, waited to see if her legs would support her, then
stood up. "Mrs. Warfield," she said, holding the counter with
one hand, straightening her shirt and fluffing her hair with
the other, "I've got a million things to do. So if you'll—"

"Now what's this stuff about a deed?" Chet interrupted.

She rubbed her temples. "My head hurts," she sighed. But
one look into those serious gray eyes told her he wasn't that
easily distracted.

"The deed, Sky...."

"Maybe you don't have enough to do over there at Four

Aces," she snapped, "what with Bud and Dale around to do all the dirty work. Maybe you ought to get a job, Chet, so you won't have so much time on your hands."

"Sky...."

"It's none of your business." Her words were strong, but her voice small and weak.

Sky's feet and hands felt as heavy as lead. "Mrs. Warfield, what do I have to do to get into my safe deposit box?"

Chet stood beside her and leaned one elbow on the counter. "Planning to sell off a section of the homestead?"

He was so close his breath rustled her hair. But she didn't dare meet his eyes because the image of the worried expression he'd worn, just moments ago as he'd held her protectively, was still too clear in her mind. Sky licked her lips. "Actually, I've been giving a new vehicle some thought."

He'd teased her once about her beat-up pickup, said she fit the small town doctor image well, right down to the broken-down jalopy. Sky heard the smile in his voice when he said, "Well, good for you."

Mrs. Warfield interrupted their conversation. "You'll have to come back this afternoon. The glue isn't dry enough to walk on yet."

The thought of Face having to spend one more minute with that madman terrified her. She'd told him the deed would be on her porch by ten o'clock. She gripped the edge of the counter and looked at the timepiece on the back wall of the teller's cage. It was nine-thirty.

"I can't wait until this afternoon!" Sky seemed unaware that her voice had taken on a shrill, hysterical quality.

The teller frowned. "You make it sound as though it's a matter of life or death." She checked her watch. "It'll only be a few hours. What's so important it can't wait that long?"

"Look, Mrs. Warfield, I mean no disrespect, but I have every right to get into that box any time during normal banking hours."

Mrs. Warfield gave Sky a scalding look over the silvery rim of her spectacles, then tilted her blue-haired head. "I'll just have another word with Mr. Harper."

"Maybe I ought to have a word with him myself," Sky muttered. She grabbed a brochure from the pocket on the counter and fanned her heated face. "Maybe I'll just tell him I'd like to withdraw my money," she said, loudly enough for Mrs. Warfield *and* Mr. Harper to hear.

Suddenly, she had an overwhelming need for a breath of fresh air, a sip of cool water. She focused on staying conscience as she followed the teller into the vault. The moment Sky had the deed in her hand she shouldered her purse and half-ran from the bank without so much as a "thank you."

"I've never known Sky to behave that way," Mrs. Warfield said, frowning. "What do you suppose it was all about?"

Chet watched through the window as Sky climbed into her truck. As though she sensed him watching, she fired it up and sped away from the curb. "Don't rightly know," Chet said. "But I aim to find out."

≈

Since he'd chosen the place, Sky insisted on being in control of the time she delivered the deed. She hadn't understood why he'd been so agreeable. In fact, his kindness made her more wary than ever. Why, he'd all but apologized for what he was doing.

But Sky had never been one to look into the mouths of gift horses. She thanked the Lord for his congeniality, sneaked out of the house while it was still dark, and hid in the pines along Route 212. From her vantage point, she'd be able to see him arrive. And when he stopped the truck and opened the door, she'd have him right where she wanted him.

Sky had taught Face to respond to a series of whistles, some that sounded like bird calls, others that more closely resembled lunchtime at a factory. The moment that he, Bart, was out of the truck, she let loose with one that meant "treats" and watched as her dog's ears pricked forward in search of its source. Sky blew again, and the Irish setter bounded toward her as Bart yelled.

"Good dog," she whispered when Face finally reached her. When the two finished saying hello, Sky checked for any signs of abuse. She remembered their last conversation, when Bart had said, "She'll be in the same shape when you get her back as she was when I borrowed her. What kind of a monster do you think I am?"

He'd sounded genuinely wounded that she'd compared him to a common crook. Sky saw no point in pointing out the obvious. She held tightly to Face's collar until Bart's truck raced back down her driveway and made a screeching entrance onto Route 212. He was no doubt in a hurry to make whatever exchange he'd had in mind when he demanded her deed in the first place.

For now, she was in the driver's seat. But her position was a precarious one, and possibly wouldn't last longer than this day. She'd have to gauge every move carefully from now on. Have to plan every step. "C'mon, girl. Let's go home."

The best attack was a surprise attack, she decided. So the moment Sky entered the house, she picked up the phone. "Martha, it's Sky. Do me a favor and spread the word: I'm closing the clinic for a while; Dr. Hammond in Lincoln City will handle emergencies." Before Martha had a chance to ask why, Sky hung up. She dialed fast and furious, calling patients and cancelling scheduled appointments. She wouldn't take the chance that he'd try another stunt like the one he'd pulled with Face while someone else's pet was on Magic

Mountain.

When she finished, Sky sat back and waited for Bart's call.

❧

She locked her truck in the garage, then headed out on foot for the place she and Wade had camped, so many summers ago.

It was a hard day's hike to the top of Boulder Pass. As she'd done with her dad, Sky started out at dawn and followed the Clearwater River west. Face trotted alongside her, stopping here and there to sniff out bear tracks and dig up miscellaneous buried treasures that she'd carry in her jaws until the next prize enticed her. Sky followed Big Hole Trail, from where Deerlodge Creek forked off to the north, across Beaverhead Plateau, and deep into Beartooth Country. Part of the beauty of this country was that it never changed. Sky recognized trees and trails that she'd marked with her Swiss army knife as a little girl, under Wade's careful supervision. Finally, as the sun slid down the back side of Granite Peak, their special place opened itself to her.

She didn't even bother to take off the heavy backpack during those first minutes of intense scrutiny. Sitting on a fallen tree trunk, hands resting on her knees and Face at her side, she drank in the territory like a woman lost in the desert might suck at the wet lip of a canteen. Not until the dog nudged her damp nose against her hand did Sky rouse from her memory trance and start the business of setting up camp.

The temperature here dipped low at night. Sometimes winds, whipping around mountain peaks, pushed the readings way below zero, even this early in the winter. But Sky had prepared herself for the weather. Mother Nature couldn't do anything to her up here to equal what the madman had done on Magic Mountain. The pup tent, poking up from the landscape like a green-handed prayer, held her supplies. If it rained, she'd climb inside; otherwise, she intended to sleep under the wide Montana sky, her faithful furry friend snuggled close beside her.

Staring up at the shimmering darkness, she felt Wade's presence. Sky barely remembered Mollie, her mother, having been only four when she left Atlanta on a sizzling August day. When she divorced Wade, she divorced Sky, too. Mollie never called or wrote, never sent presents or cards. She'd been on the road with Bobbie Jones and his Steel Guitar Band for three years when their van ran off the road during a Minnesota blizzard. Mollie's mother called Wade with the news on what would have been their tenth anniversary. He spent a long time alone in his room that night.

Wade more than made up for Sky's lack of a mom. Being sheriff, he could often whittle time in his workday to accompany her on field trips. He never missed a school pageant or a parent/teacher conference, and occasionally showed up in the school cafeteria carrying a bag full of Big Jim's burgers for Sky and her friends. He taught her how to find her way through a dense forest, where to find drinking water, and how to tell which berries and mushrooms were poisonous, so she could survive in any locale. Out behind the sheriff's department, he taught her to load and shoot a pistol, a rifle, a shotgun; he taught her to respect not only the weapons but the power behind them as well.

He loved bluegrass music and opera, Shakespeare and Twain, grits and escargot, and, in his excitement to experience life, he taught her to accept and be tolerant, to find enjoyment in the very things that made people individuals.

Wade liked to alter trite clichés. "Never met a kid I didn't like," he'd say, putting a new twist on the famous line. And like a six-foot-high magnet, he attracted children of all shapes and sizes everywhere he went, dispensing quarters for phone calls home and dollar bills for the ice cream man.

Sky missed Wade more at that moment than she'd missed him in those first hard days after he was shot. He'd have known how to handle the crazy man in the hills. And he'd have told her how to fix the mess of things she'd made with Chet. She snuggled deep into the down-stuffed sleeping bag. *They'd have gotten along famously,* she thought, missing them both more than she cared to admit.

That night, with her heart and head full of wonderful Wade memories, she slept deeply and peacefully for the first time in months. When she woke at dawn, she felt as though she'd slept six nights instead of one and she sat up to stretch and breathe in the pure sharp scent of spruce. Immediately, she got onto her knees and faced the sun. "Dear Lord," she prayed, hands folded and face tilted toward the heavens, "thank You for a night of peaceful slumber. Thank You for this glorious morning. For this beautiful view. For all You've given me. Bless this day and make me do Your will throughout it. Amen."

When she was finished, Face gave her a good morning doggy grin and wagged her tail. "You like it up here, don't you, girl?" Sky asked, ruffling the dog's thick russet coat. A quick, wet slurp across the cheek was Sky's answer. Laughing, she said, "How 'bout some breakfast?"

After rolling up her sleeping bag, Sky poked at the smoldering campfire. Carefully, she placed dried leaves and sticks atop the coals and blew gently across it until they glowed red. When the tiny flames licked at the twigs, she added bigger and bigger limbs, until the fire blazed hot and bright. She dumped two teaspoons of coffee grounds into the bottom of the blue-speckled percolator and poured fresh mountain spring water on top of them. While she waited for it to bubble, Sky emptied a pouch of dog food onto a metal plate. "There you go," she told the dog. "Eat up; we have a big day ahead."

Her own breakfast consisted of two strips of beef jerky and a crisp apple, washed down by hot black coffee. When she finished eating, Sky splashed icy water from a nearby stream onto her face and brushed her teeth. Piling the rocks higher around the campfire to prevent sparks from igniting nearby brush, Sky grabbed her rifle and her mess kit and headed north, toward the place Wade had dubbed "Bit o' Heaven." It took an hour to hike the dusty gritty trail; Sky presumed she and Wade had been the last to tramp there.

When she finally reached the top, tears stung her eyes as she surveyed the pristine scene. "How anyone could plant their boots on ground like this and say they don't believe in God is beyond me!" Wade would say. Sky couldn't help but agree, for only a powerful and mighty being could have created anything so vast and magnificent. The vista was an explosion of color and scent, from the sunlit mountain peaks to the twisting blue river below, from the pale azure sky to the pillowy green of the faraway tree tops.

An eagle screamed overhead as a fuzzy white mountain goat skittered down a rocky slope, her kid close on her heels. Cottony clouds sailed silently by, so close it seemed, she could reach up and touch them. Sky stared with pride at the pink snow that dappled the mountaintop, knowing that she could count on one hand the number of places in the world where the stuff existed. Bit o' Heaven had certainly earned its name.

Face lifted her head and sniffed the wind, familiarizing herself with the odors of the wilderness. Moose and bear, bison and pronghorn shared the place with geese and ptarmigan and saw-whet owls. In the spring, nodding yellowbells and shooting stars made way for summer's daisies and fall's wild mums. Sapphires, garnets, and smoky quartz hid beneath the rich soil.

Here, a ghost town, there, a mining town. No matter which way Sky looked, she felt the life that was this land. *A few days here,* she thought, *will make things right again.*

Sky waited until the sun disappeared before she picked her way back down the trail to her camp. Big broad pawprints in the dirt around the campfire told her she'd had an uninvited guest. Storing her food in airtight metal canisters had been the only thing that stood between the bear's curious visit and total destruction of the campsite. Smiling, Sky laid her rifle on the ground, sat on the cold hard earth, and leaned back against a nearby tree trunk. At lunchtime, she'd given half her mustard and bologna sandwich to Face; despite her long hike, Sky wasn't the least bit hungry. "Maybe we'll dig out the old liverwurst when it gets dark," she told the dog. Face woofed at the mention of her favorite treat. Feeling lazy and tranquilized, Sky closed her eyes, her hands folded loosely in her lap, and dozed. Only when the chill of the night set in did she rouse, and then only, long enough to unroll her sleeping bag and climb inside.

The next day's sunrise looked even more spectacular than the first. But as she watched the yellow sphere blot out the darkness on the third morning, she knew it was time to return to Magic Mountain. Though Sky loved life on the mountaintop, three days without a proper bath were about as many as she could take. Face loped along ahead of her, following their three-day-old scents, and Sky grinned. "We'll make a mountain dog out of you yet," she called ahead. Face, at the sound of her mistress' voice, turned and galloped toward her, ran a happy circle around Sky, then dashed back down the trail. When she got back to the house, Sky decided, she'd shower and change and invite Dale to meet her for supper in Mountain Gate.

❧

The house reminded Sky of a pancake syrup label. Old-fashioned and inviting, it popped onto the horizon like a welcome home sign, its wide porch like open arms that waited to greet each visitor with a big warm hug. She remembered feeling the very same way at the start of each summer. The moment Wade turned his big red truck into Magic Mountain's entrance, anticipation and elation combined to such a level of impatience that Sky would inevitably be bouncing up and down on the seat by the time he parked in front of the double-doored garage. She felt that same itchy eagerness now and quickened her step until she'd broken into a full run, thirty-pound backpack and all. Sky reached the porch feeling breathless but invigorated and sat on the bottom step to catch her breath and scan the view.

Behind her on the porch, Face whimpered, then barked. Sky turned to see what had caused the dog's unusual behavior. Face was growling and pawing at something on the floor, and Sky slipped the backpack from her shoulders. "What's up, girl?" she asked, climbing the stairs. "Did you find another chipmunk?"

Gran had always insisted that her porch floor gleam with bright, white enamel. There, in the middle of those milky wood planks, he'd painted a message in bold, blood-red letters: *Gonna have a hot time on the old town tonight!*

seventeen

Dale had been asking her for weeks to have dinner with him. She'd said yes, but only because she believed it was the only way to make him stop pestering her. He'd always been able to make her feel good, no matter what. And, despite all that was going on in her life, he'd made her laugh and smile.

Still, she was tired and a little sad when she came home after dinner to the big empty house, for she knew no message from Chet would be waiting on her machine. And there'd be no chance whatever that he'd drop by to say hello…to warn her to be careful…to tease her about baking mountains of chocolate chip cookies.

Because he was gone.

Dale had told her he'd left for Wyoming two days ago. "He always heads north when things start eatin' at him," her friend said. "Sometimes he stays a few days, sometimes a month or more."

Sky sighed. She'd probably never see Chet again. And just because it was best for all concerned didn't make it easier to bear.

Sky dropped onto the sofa. Something cool touched her cheek. Immediately, she knew what it was: Chet's tie. Sky snuggled against it, letting the smooth silk caress her skin. She sat up and, holding one end in each hand, studied the navy cloth. Impulsively, Sky gathered it in her palms, held it to her face, and closed her eyes. Tears squeezed from their corners as she inhaled its fresh masculine scent.

Face knew better than to leap onto the couch, yet risked a scolding to comfort her mistress. Whimpering, she licked the backs of Sky's hands, then sniffed the tie.

Sky hugged her, overlooking that she'd broken a house rule. "I miss him, too," she admitted. She didn't fight the tears. Couldn't, it seemed. Soon, Face's fur clumped where Sky's teardrops fell in a steady stream.

Long after the crying jag ended and the Irish setter's fur had dried, Gran's clock chimed ten o'clock...then eleven o'clock. At the stroke of midnight, Sky headed for her bedroom. She never expected to sleep but, after an hour of tossing and turning, she did.

Suddenly, she woke with a start; Face's bark had awakened her. The clock on the nightstand said 2:38. The only other time she'd heard Face bark so ferociously had been on the day they'd found the cubs. The dog ran back and forth in front of the window, stopping every few seconds to look outside.

"What is it, girl?" Sky asked, running to the window. But even before she got there, Sky knew the answer—fire!

The air was full of the unmistakable odor of burning wood. Outside, the sky was bright with the yellow-orange flames that lapped at the clinic's porch. Knowing she didn't have a minute to waste, she grabbed the phone as she stepped into her boots. Instead of the customary *buzz* of the dial tone, Sky heard nothing. The silence was deafening...terrifying... deadly.

She knew better than to let Face go out there, and slammed the bedroom door behind her, trapping the dog inside. Face's high-pitched barks rang in her ears as she raced across the lawn, glad she hadn't had time to put the garden hose into the shed. Sky turned the water on full blast, grabbed the nozzle end of the hose, and aimed it at the clinic's porch, where the blaze burned brightest. Fortunately, the fire seemed contained to this one area; if she could get it under control quickly enough, maybe it wouldn't spread.

For half an hour, the flames struggled to survive, sizzling

under the steady stream of water, then died with a sputter. Finally, when the last spark dimmed, Sky sat in a murky puddle on the bottom step, soaked and shivering in the cold night air, her face sooty and her hair singed, still holding the spurting hose in one trembling hand. She heard Face, barking inside, and hoped the frantic dog hadn't torn up her room too badly. Weak from fear and tension, she twisted the nozzle to stop the water's flow and then dropped the hose. Holding her head in her hands, she thought of the first wolf discussion she and Chet had had in the wee hours of the morning, days after she'd found the cubs.

"Leaving them out there might have been the most humane thing you could have done," he'd said. For a moment, she wondered if two wild animals were worth all this misery. Then she pictured their shaggy silver coats and big clumsy paws and round golden eyes. They were worth it, all right…and then some.

Shakily, she stood, holding tightly to the porch railing for support. Something crinkled beneath her sooty palm; Sky grabbed it. Another message, she realized, from her pen pal. Instantly, she knew why it had been such a small, contained fire: He'd set it to tell her, in no uncertain terms, exactly what he was capable of. "Next time," she read aloud, "I won't give you time to react." Sky folded the note and tucked it into the back pocket of her jeans, remembering that first note. She realized she'd never gotten around to getting it back from Chet. She missed him more at that moment than she ever had.

By now he must be in Wyoming, trying to forget her.

She headed for the house, but stopped in the middle of the front yard and faced Granite Peak. "I have nothing more to lose," she screamed. Though she hollered for all she was worth, her voice seemed small and weak in the vast Montana sky. "Go ahead, you coward! Give me your best shot!" She spread her arms wide, making herself an easy target; hoping her actions would prove to him that nothing he did from now on could hurt her.

Minutes ticked silently by.

"Coward!" she shouted again, then turned on her heel and climbed onto the porch, where she sat down and calmly removed her wet boots. Placing them beside the door, she went inside and didn't even bother to lock it.

Face ran from the bedroom the moment Sky opened the door. Sky ignored her and fell into bed, exhausted, and buried her face in the pillow. Within minutes, she was asleep.

Sky woke at noon, no less tired than when she'd gone to bed. She was cold and wet, to boot, but she climbed into the truck and drove into Mountain Gate. She needed lumber and nails to repair the damage from the fire.

She stacked her supplies on a skid beside the counter. "What's that?" Martha asked, reaching out to touch a smudge on Sky's cheek. "Why, it's soot," the old woman confirmed.

"A little cold for a barbecue," Dale said, using his bandanna to wipe her cheek.

Her heart fluttered. If she told them what had happened, they'd rally to her side. And then she'd have two more loved ones to worry about. She was still determined not to risk anyone else's safety on account of her decision to raise those cubs.

"Oh," she began, "I foolishly forgot to turn off the coffeepot in the clinic. Guess it shorted out during the night. Started a little fire. No big deal."

"No big deal," Dale repeated, looking stern and parental.

"Really. It's all under control," she said, grinning to prove things were fine. "A little damage to the railing, but I'll have it fixed in no time," she added, pointing to the lumber.

Dale's blue eyes narrowed. "You have a power saw?" Sky nodded yes.

"And a hammer?"

"Gramps had a fully equipped tool shed, remember?" Dale and Sky had built a treehouse one summer. It had been such a resounding success that they'd tried their hands at a row-boat the following year. Though the boat didn't survive even one dip in Gibson's pond, the treehouse was still standing.

Dale tucked in one corner of his mouth. "How could I forget?" Affectionately, he pushed a wayward red curl behind her ear. "Be careful, y'hear? 'Cause I also remember you have a tendency to hit more thumbs than nails."

He shot a strange, worried look at Martha, who, contrary to her personality and character, said nothing.

Sky held her fake confident grin in place. "These are the hands of a surgeon now," she said, thumbs up.

The moment she was out of sight, Dale turned to Martha. "I need your phone."

"Why don't you call Chet," the old woman said. "Maybe he can talk some sense into our girl."

He'd vowed not to dial the Wyoming number, knowing how much Chet had needed the time alone. But what choice did he have now? Sky's stubborn streak had turned one of her most admirable character traits into a potentially deadly threat. Dale knew if anyone could make her admit it, Chet could. He waded through the obligatory small talk with Chet's mom and, when she handed the phone to her son, decided Sky's nonchalant attitude would be the most effective approach.

"She's fine and says the clinic wasn't damaged badly. But that fire didn't start because of any coffeepot. I've known her nearly all my life and I can tell when she's not telling the whole truth. Besides, she said the porch was the only thing damaged. The coffeepot's clear on the other side of the clinic!"

"Must be fifteen feet between that cart and the door," Chet agreed.

"Exactly. She told me she got another message, too. The guy had left it painted right on her porch floor. She found it when she got back from her camping trip."

"What camping trip?"

"Up on Beartooth. She got back the day before you left. Stayed up there three days…longest she's been out there alone since her daddy died."

Chet's heart beat hard and fast with concern. He pictured Beartooth Plateau, as wild and dangerous as it was beautiful. "What'd she go up there for? The bears are meaner just before hibernation than any other. Sky knows that. What could she have been thinking?"

"I don't think she *was* thinking," Dale said. "She went up there for the same reason you're in Wyoming." He almost said "love," then thought better of it. "She's crazy about you, big guy."

"She's sure got a funny way of showing it."

"That's Sky for you. Putting the safety of her loved ones ahead of her own."

Chet cleared his throat, remembering that scene on her porch when she'd gone from warm and loving to cold and bitter in a heartbeat. Suddenly, it all made sense. She'd picked that fight to protect *him*!

"I can be there by sundown if I leave right now," Chet said. "But don't you tell a soul I'm coming back. I want to catch that…I want to catch him with my bare hands."

"You got it."

"Thanks, Dale."

"Aw, now don't go gettin' all mushy on me. Just get back here. Fast."

His mother had been standing in the doorway, blatantly eavesdropping. "This Sky," she said as he hung up the phone, "is she the same Dr. Allen that Sally talks about nonstop?"

Chet nodded and refilled his coffee cup.

Lucy sat at the table. "Park it, son."

He took the seat across from her and watched that left brow rise on her forehead, a sure sign that he was in for a lecture.

"You love her, you big galoot. Why, it's as plain as the nose on your face. Why is that so hard to admit?"

. Chet ran one big finger round and round the rim of his cup. "I've asked myself that question a thousand times."

"Loyalty."

He met the eyes so like his own, though a few more laugh lines crinkled at their corners. "Loyalty?"

"For Ella." Lucy patted her son's hand. "She's been gone a long time, son. I know how much you miss her. I miss her, too." She pursed her lips and tilted her head, causing her silver-streaked bangs to fall over one gray eye. "I came to think of her as a daughter in the years you two were together. She was a spectacular woman."

Chet smiled sadly.

"What do you suppose she'd say if she knew you had a chance at happiness, but passed it up because of some long dead memory?"

He blinked and said nothing. He'd never given the matter a moment's thought. Why would he, when no woman but Sky had ever touched his heart as Ella had?

Lucy sighed. "All right. I'll put it another way. If it had been you who had died, would you want Ella spending the rest of her life alone? Unloved? Clinging to cold memories?"

"Of course not!" he bellowed. "I'd want her to—"

"To be happy?"

"Yes," he whispered. "I'd want that more than anything."

Just as she'd done when he was a boy, Lucy let silence teach the final lesson. After a wordless moment, she got up and refilled her coffee cup. "Sky must be some woman to have turned your head."

He'd been absent-mindedly picking at the tiny nubs on the red-checkered tablecloth. Chet looked up when she said that and smiled into eyes that were mirror images of his own. "She's that, all right."

"But she's nothing like Ella. Is that what scares you so much?"

The smile vanished. As always, Lucy had zeroed in on his

biggest concern. It was true; he and Sky were exact opposites. He'd always been attracted to petite women. Blonds, in particular, with big blue eyes and soft, womanly curves. "She's nearly as tall as me, Ma, with flaming red hair and brown eyes as big as your saucer, there. And stubborn...." Chet whistled. "Strong as an ox, too. And independent to a fault." *But more woman than any I've known in my lifetime,* he added, mentally.

"Ella was just a slip of a girl when you two married. And you weren't much more than a boy, yourself. But you're a grown man, now and balancing big responsibilities on those shoulders of yours," she said, a teasing glint in her eyes. "Sally...the ranch...all those cowhands. And Stella is a handful, all by herself!" Lucy laughed. Then, sighing again, she added, "Your pa would be so proud of you."

He looked at her with new eyes and saw not just his mother, but a beautiful woman. A woman who had been cherished and loved for nearly a quarter of a century by one man...his father. "Why didn't you take your own advice?"

She returned to the chair as a dreamy, loving light put a youthful sparkle in her eyes. "You mean, why didn't I remarry?"

Chet nodded.

"Because I'm a fool, to put it plainly. Happiness came my way once but, like you, I thought grasping it would be disloyal; that the world might think I didn't really love your pa." Her wistful smile shrank as she added, "Yes, I came close.... He was a wonderful, patient man. Moaned around like a lost pup for years."

"Not Jesse Coolidge!"

"One and the same. One day he realized life was passing him by. He told me he didn't have an eternity to wait for me to come to my senses." She'd been staring off into space as she talked, focused on some point in time only she could see.

She grabbed his hand suddenly. "Don't be like your mama,

son. Love like that doesn't come along every day. Don't let it slip through your fingers."

Ᏸ

Their conversation had given Chet a later start than he'd planned, but Lucy's advice traveled with him all the way back to Mountain Gate. Suddenly, he understood that what had attracted him to Sky in the first place had been the very things he admired most in his mother—inner strength, common sense, love that knew no bounds and for which no sacrifice was too great.

His mother had insisted on keeping Sally with her in Wyoming, saying she'd bring the child and his vehicle home when life in Montana seemed safe and normal again. "It's about time for me to give that mother-in-law of yours another dose of reality anyway," she'd said, winking. Lucy had also insisted that he drive her car, not his truck, back to Mountain Gate.

"Keep that crazy man guessing," she'd said when she kissed him goodbye. And then she'd handed him a roll of shelf paper and told him to cover Sky's garage windows the minute he'd parked the Caddy inside.

After he'd told her everything that had been going on, Lucy had suggested he move into Sky's house to protect her. "And don't take no for an answer," she'd said. "I suspect it's not what Sky wants to hear, anyway."

Chet switched off the headlights, then drove as slowly and quietly down Sky's driveway as possible. Luckily, he found the garage doors open and he pulled the Cadillac alongside her pickup truck. Once the place was shut up tight, the only means of entry was the narrow Dutch door centered in the back wall. Then Chet set about the task of covering the windows with the paper and tape his mother had given him, grabbed his duffle bag, and sneaked out the back door, locking it behind him.

As he walked across the snow-dusted grass, he heard Face

barking inside the darkened house. The dog was one of the most well-behaved setters he'd ever seen; it was unlike her to carry on like that. Chet couldn't help wondering what task occupied Sky so completely that she hadn't done anything to hush the noisy barking.

The hood of her truck had been cold, telling him that she hadn't driven it for hours at least. Without it, there were few places she'd go on foot. He hoped she hadn't headed for the hills again. But an even scarier thought flitted through his mind: What if the madman who'd been tormenting her had gotten into the house?

Worry and fear made his heart beat hard and fast and Chet broke into a run. He was on the porch in seconds, jiggling the doorknob and banging on the front door. When it swung open at his touch, icy fear flowed through him.

He stepped cautiously into the gloomy foyer.

"Sky!" he called.

Face stopped barking suddenly and he wondered what…or who…had stopped her. The silence was at once terrifying and deafening.

"Sky! Where are you?"

Chet stepped hesitantly into the darkened living room. All the dread he'd been accumulating faded when he saw her snuggled beneath her favorite afghan. *Thank you, Lord,* he prayed silently. *Thank you….*

She looked tired, small, and so vulnerable lying there on the couch. Chet's heartbeat returned to a more normal pace as he strode toward her.

He sat on the edge of the sofa, prepared to take her in his arms, wake her, and tell her how much he'd missed her and how much he loved her . Then Face entered the room, tail wagging and mouth yapping in a happy greeting for her pal, Chet.

Surely she heard that, he told himself, frowning.

But Sky didn't stir.

"Sky," he said, shaking her. "Sky, wake up...."

Groggily, she sat up and rubbed her eyes. It took her a moment to focus. Chet noticed the bottle of over-the-counter sleeping pills on the table beside her.

"How many of these have you taken?" he insisted.

Sky squinted and put her hand beside her head. "What?"

He was really worried now. What if all that had been happening to her had finally caused her to snap. What if she'd....

"What were you thinking?" he thundered, standing and grabbing the bottle from the table.

She tucked her hair behind her ears and nonchalantly removed two foam earplugs. "What are you hollering about? Say...how did you get in here?" she asked, suddenly aware of his presence. "I don't recall giving you a key...."

"The door wasn't locked."

That stunned her and she screwed up her face in honest confusion. "Guess I was more exhausted than I realized."

"I'll ask you one more time," he said, thrusting the medicine bottle in her face, "how many of these did you take?"

"Just one...as if that's any of you business." She crossed both arms over her chest. "What are you doing here?"

He opened his mouth to answer, and the doorbell chimed.

"Neat trick," she said, grinning.

"Ignoring her, Chet headed for the foyer and peeked onto the porch. "You've got company," he said through clenched teeth.

Sky rose and joined him. "What's *he* doing here ?" she whispered.

"Why don't you just find out." He headed for the kitchen. "I'll be in here, in case you need me...."

eighteen

When Sky opened the door, Bart stepped, uninvited, into the foyer. "I know I should have called first," he said, removing his Stetson, "but I was afraid you wouldn't see me."

Sky closed the door behind him. She followed his gaze to where two plates of cake and two glasses of milk stood on the coffee table. "I was just having a little snack. Can I get you something?"

Bart shook his head. "No, thanks." He seemed agitated; his nervousness confused and frightened Sky.

"Can I sit down for a minute?" He walked into the living room and flopped into her easy chair. "I don't know where to begin," he said, holding his head in his hands.

Though she'd known him most of her life, for the most part, Sky had avoided Bart Laurence. She couldn't quite figure out why, except to quote Gran: "He gives me the heebie-jeebies." Sky sent a silent prayer of thanks that Chet was in the kitchen, where he'd gone at the sound of the door bell.

"Have you been drinking?" she asked Bart.

He met her eyes. "No. I'm sober as a judge." He took a deep breath. "This is…this is going to be hard…."

Sky sat on the end of the couch farthest from him. "I'm sorry, Sky," he said, turning his hat round and round in his hands. "It's been horrible, and I'm sorry."

A nervous giggle popped from her mouth. "Sorry for what, Bart?"

Staring at an invisible spot between his boots, he shook his head. "It was me. All of it. I have no excuse…no good excuse, that is." Briefly, he met Sky's eyes. Then, shaking his head again, he placed his hat on the cushioned arm of the chair. Focusing on the enlarged photograph of Granite Peak, he repeated, more softly this time, "I'm sorry."

Sky leaped from the couch. "You mean…. The shots? Face? The calls and the notes…and the fire…." Her eyes were wide with fright. "That was…all of that was *you*?"

Bart sighed and nodded. "It's a long story."

Sky pulled herself together and sat on the sofa's arm. "I have plenty of time," she said coolly, crossing her legs and arms at the same time.

Bart took a deep breath. "Maybe I'll take you up on your offer after all," he said, his voice shaking. Timidly, he met her eyes. "Could I…? How about a glass of water…?"

Half an hour later, he'd spelled the whole thing out. "If you want to call the sheriff, I won't put up a fight." Taking another deep breath, he added, "I'm sorry. I'm so sorry."

Chet walked into the room. "Sorry doesn't cut it, Laurence."

Bart shook his head and showed Chet his palms. He didn't seem the least bit surprised to see Chet there. "You can shoot me later, Cozart," he said. "Right now, we have more important things to do. We have to figure out how we're going to stop Rowen and save Sky's land."

She sat straight and tall, her chin high and her lips a taut line. Chet was proud of her strength and assurance. Not until he sat beside her and grabbed her trembling hand did he realize that the whole thing was for Bart's benefit.

"You mean how we're going to stop Rowen and save the Lazy L?" Chet injected, reminding them all that Bart had admitted having handed over the deed to his ranch during a drunken game of poker.

"Can't blame you one whit for not believing me," Bart said. "But I'm on the level."

Chet harumphed the statement. "You say you have an idea how we can help Sky?"

"Yeah. I do. But somebody could get hurt."

Sky's dark eyes asked the silent question: *Can we trust you?*

Bart thought of the conversation he'd overheard in Rowen's waiting room…of the man who died in the so called drunk driving accident. A look of fear and disgust crossed his face. "Believe me, I have as much to lose as you do."

Bart gave them a moment to ponder his statement. "Look," he said, "we have to act fast. He's like a locomotive and he'll flatten anybody who gets in his way. The only way to beat him is to play by his rules."

"What's with all this 'we' stuff?" Chet demanded. "Play? Rules? This isn't a game, Bart."

Bart's folded hands dangled between his knees. "Maybe not," he countered, "but there can only be one winner in this mess." He looked at Sky for a moment, then back at Chet before adding, "I'd kinda like it to be Sky, wouldn't you?"

They had no reason to trust him, he admitted. No reason to believe he was really on their side. "Consider the alternative," Bart suggested. Shrugging, he smiled slightly. "You don't have much choice, as I see it."

Chet was on his feet in a heartbeat. "One phone call," he grated through clenched teeth, "and you'll be behind bars so fast it'll shock the scales off those snakeskin boots of yours."

· Sky grabbed the clenched fist nearest her. "Wait a minute," she said. "I hate to interrupt all this macho confrontational stuff, but somebody has to be the voice of reason."

Chet glared at her for a moment, then softened and returned to his seat beside her. He slipped a possessive, protective arm around her waist. "So what's the voice of reason saying?" he asked, grinning crookedly.

Her mouth became a taut, thin line before she said, "I think he's on the level. Why else would he come here?"

Chet's grin died instantly as he faced Bart again. "It could be a trick. Get us off guard so he can get in another whack."

Sky shook her head.

Frowning, he looked at her again. "Are you crazy?" Chet spat. "He's been tormenting you for months, and just because he ambles in here with his tail between his legs, you think he's turned into a good guy all of a sudden?"

"Yes," she said simply.

Chet clucked his tongue and rolled his eyes. "Oh, sure," he said under his breath.

Suddenly, he remembered that Bart still sat in the chair across the room. Coughing, he squared his shoulders. "All right. So we'll do it his way." Then, facing his opponent, he glowered and jabbed his forefinger in the air. "But I'm gonna have my eye on you, buster. One false move and…."

Bart nodded. "Fine. Whatever you say. In fact, when this is over, you've got my permission to beat me senseless. Now, can we get busy?"

It was nearly midnight before Bart finally left them alone again. The three of them had finished off two pots of coffee and the chocolate cake before they'd come up with a dangerous, but not impossible plan.

nineteen

"I hoe art ish kee-in' Owen izzy."

Sky's hands froze above the file drawer as she replayed Chet's sentence in her mind. When it still made absolutely no sense, she whispered, "What?"

"I hoe art ish kee-in' Owen izzy."

She looked at Chet, hunched over the tall metal filing cabinet on the other side of the darkened room. If not for the small flashlight he held between his teeth to illuminate the contents of the drawer, Sky wouldn't have been able to see him at all, since he wore nothing but black, from his long-sleeved shirt to his high-topped sneakers. Only the brown knit gloves kept him from fitting the super-spy image he'd tried so hard to duplicate.

Sky looked like a shadow, too, wearing a snug black jumpsuit over a black turtleneck. "Take that penlight out of your mouth," she said, grinning at his murky form. "I can't understand a word you're saying."

His quiet laughter echoed in the file drawer. "Uh, sorry." He grabbed the light and repeated, "I hope Bart is keeping Rowen busy."

"Me, too." Her heart thudded with fear. What if someone discovered them there in Rowen's office suite? The frightening possibilities were endless. Unfortunately, to beat Rowen at his own game, they were forced to play by his rules.

The night Bart had surprised them with a visit, he told them he had proof that Rowen had been paying a prominent Montana senator big bucks to falsify licenses and permits. Once he'd confessed to his part in the scheme to get Sky's land, Bart told them how he'd sneaked Rowen's keys from the office just long enough to make copies. Sky and Chet had already photocopied those incriminating documents, and put the originals back exactly as they'd found them.

At the moment, they searched for evidence that would prove Rowen never intended to turn the mountain into a wildlife preserve, as the paperwork outlined. Government grants and tax-free incentives encouraged the nation's well-intentioned wealthy to invest in the environment. What Rowen really had planned for Granite Peak would preserve nothing but his huge bank account. Once the deeds changed hands, it would cost the state of Montana billions of dollars in court costs to prevent Rowen from doing whatever he wanted with his mountain. Bart's apology preceded his admission that he'd do whatever it took to help Sky and Chet stop Rowen before things ever got that far.

So that very next morning, while Sky drove Face to Four Aces, where she'd stay with Dale, Chet booked them on the first flight out of Butte. Immediately after landing at Baltimore Washington International Airport, they rented a boxy black sedan.

The plan demanded they work under cover of darkness. Since they'd arrived hours ahead of schedule, Sky and Chet killed time, chatting like ordinary tourists in the long line at Phillip's Restaurant, famous from Maine to Florida for its seafood.

After dinner, they walked arm in arm, admiring the gigantic blue fluorescent wave that was the Aquarium's trademark, and the gleaming sailboats and yachts docked near the brick promenade.

"One for the lady?" asked a young boy.

Chet exchanged dollar bills for a long-stemmed red rose

from the boy's basket, then bowed low as he handed it to Sky.

"It's beautiful," she said.

"It pales in comparison to you."

Now, in Rowen's fancy office suite near the top of the World Trade Center, she could see the colorful lights of the Inner Harbor below. The glittering scene reminded her of the brief but dazzling kiss they'd exchanged before entering the sky-scraper.

"How're you doin'?"

His question forced Sky to concentrate on the task at hand. "Well," she whispered into the darkness, "considering there appears to be thousands of folders in here, I guess I'm making progress. I've gone through two file cabinets so far. How 'bout you?"

Eyes on his work, Chet said, "I'm nearly finished with my second cabinet, too." He grunted, then added, "Any luck?"

"Not yet. But we still have at least ten cabinets to snoop through."

"I'm beginning to wonder if we're going to find anything at all. I'll bet Bart was just giving us—"

"Now, be fair," she interrupted. "He did get us those keys, don't forget. And everything else he told us has been on target, too. Let's see what we find here before we loop the hangman's noose around his neck."

Grinning, he said, "Get back to work, will you?"

The only sound in the gloomy room was the quiet shuffling of papers as their fingers walked through file after file. Suddenly, Chet yanked a folder from the drawer and said, "Eureka!"

&

They'd been sitting side by side in the front seat of the rental car for nearly fifteen minutes, chatting casually as they waited for Bart to join them when Chet said, "I think we should get a new place once we're married."

Sky couldn't believe her ears. *Married?* she repeated mentally. "But…my patients…?"

"Mountain Gate isn't New York City, sweet stuff," he said, kissing her temple. "They'll find you. Trust me."

And she did trust him. Completely. Smiling happily, Sky turned in the seat to face him. "Why are we discussing where we'll live when we've never even said how we feel about one another?"

He looked deep into her eyes.

Grinning, she shook her head.

"But…I just called you 'sweet stuff'…Well, you haven't said it, either. Ladies first, and all that."

Sky frowned. Then, squinting, she stared through the windshield at the stars that dappled the velvety black sky. "Let's compromise. No good marriage can survive without it."

He draped his arm over her shoulders. "Start talking."

"No. We'll *both* start talking. *That's* the compromise. On the count of three."

Chet opened his mouth, indicating his readiness to comply.

"One, two, three…. I love you!" she said alone.

"That's the meanest, scariest look anybody ever gave me!" He grinned, then squeezed her shoulder.

"You cheated!"

He spoke slowly: "But…I've asked you…to marry me."

"Not in so many words."

The thick mustache tilted teasingly.

"It's easy. I love you," she demonstrated. "I love you. I love you. I love you."

"I love you," he said softly.

No three words had ever sounded better. "Was it really so hard?"

He leaned back and sighed, then hugged her. "I do, you know. Always have. Right from the moment your fist connected with my eye…love at first fight," he said, accenting the first letter of the last word.

"Ditto."

"Didn't know you spoke Morse Code," he teased.

"That's what we'll name our first son!"

"Like that comic strip kid? I won't hear of it."

"No, silly. Not Ditto. Morse."

"No son of mine is gonna have a name that rhymes with horse." He held her closer. "Our *first* son? How many sons are you planning to give me?"

"Two. But I won't *give* them to you. I'll just let you borrow them from time to time, so you can show off in front of all the other cowboys. They'll be *my* sons. Maybe you can have the girls."

His eyes glittered with amusement. "And how many of those will you give me?"

"One."

"Only one?"

"You already have a daughter. Don't be greedy."

❧

Bart took the seat nearest the window. "Sorry," he said. "I'm not used to thinking of other people first. Would one of you like to sit here?" he asked, rising as far from the seat as the airplane's overhead compartment would allow.

Sky grinned and sat beside him. "Stay where you are," she said, patting the hand that rested on her shoulder.

He glanced at her delicate, pale hand atop his dark, weathered one, and repressed the urge to grab it, hold it tightly, and press a long, meaningful kiss on it. He pulled down his seat tray and opened his dog-eared paperback novel. "Thanks," he said quietly.

Two hours into the flight, as Bart snored softly, Chet whispered into her ear, "He's got it bad for you, girl."

It was precisely what Dale had said when she'd thought she'd lost Chet. Her heart ached with the mere remembrance of it. "Don't be silly."

That left brow rose slowly on his forehead. "Silly?" he repeated. His bent forefinger lifted her chin and gray eyes bored deeply into hers. "I know what I'm talking about." His lips were nearly touching her ear when he added, "That look on his face…. I saw it in the mirror for months."

Sky gasped. "But…. But I never…. I didn't…."

"You didn't have to do anything, sweet stuff," he said. "You just had to be you." Chet kissed her lovingly. "And stop looking so guilty. Loving you is what turned his life around."

She started to protest, but his finger, pressed gently to her lips, silenced her. "I know what I'm talking about," he said again.

Sky listened to the soft, steady breaths of the man snoozing contentedly beside her, the man who, only days ago, had been an unknown, fearsome enemy. Who only last night had put his life on the line for her and Magic Mountain. Leaning her head on Chet's shoulder, she sighed.

"What's going on in that pretty head of yours?" Chet asked.

"I'm just wondering what'll become of him. When we get back to Mountain Gate, I mean."

Chet slid his arm behind her and pulled her close. "He's got a chance to fly straight now," he said. "You gave him that chance." Kissing her temple, he added, "It's up to him from here on out."

❧

Chet counted the charges on his fingers: "Bribing public officials; falsifying court documents; fraud; extortion; the list goes on and on," he said, smiling as he watched Rowen sift through the file he and Sky had made.

Rown tanned face paled as the practiced smile vanished. "Where did you get this?" he demanded, tossing the folder onto the desk.

Bart had been leaning casually against the wall, precisely where Hugo usually stood, studying his fingernails. "From right under your uppity nose, Rowen," he said, his voice dripping with sarcasm.

Mike Rowen glared at each of them. "I oughta call the cops." He jumped up and began pacing in front of the window wall, hands clasped behind him. "I oughta have the lot of you arrested, that's what I oughta do," he said, his voice devoid of its former skilled spokesman's tone, "for breaking and entering...burglary...invasion of privacy."

Bart calmly inspected the toothpick he'd been chewing and nonchalantly asked, "Where's your evidence?" He looked at the file folder. "In there?"

Rowen's fists opened and closed, opened and closed. "You're lucky I'm not a violent man."

Suddenly, Bart crossed the room and filled his hands with Rowen's lapels. "You're not going to do anything to anybody, because if you so much as think about it, I'll...."

"Bart," Sky said, "let go of him."

Confusion widened his eyes. "He was willing to do anything to get your land. *Anything*, Sky. How can you defend him?"

She placed her hand on his forearm. "I'm not defending him. I'm defending you."

Brown eyes fused to blue as their wills battled. In a moment, the fury in Bart's eyes abated. "All right. I'll let him go. But if it were up to me," he snapped, tossing Rowen back and setting him free, "I'd string him up from the nearest lamp post."

Rowen jerked his jaw left and right, then straightened his tie in an attempt to reclaim lost dignity. "I suppose you cowpokes have made copies of that …."

Chet nodded and grinned. "Yup," he drawled, "and you'll get 'em back when you hand over the deed to Bart's land."

Rowen slumped into the red leather chair on the visitors' side of the desk and faced Chet. "How do I know I can trust you?"

Shrugging, he said, "Well, pardner, I guess you don't."

The standoff lasted a long, uncomfortable moment. Then Rowen reached into the inner pocket of his gaberdine suitcoat and removed the envelope that held the deed to the Lazy L. He tossed it on the floor at Bart's feet. "He's no friend of yours, Dr. Allen," he hissed, facing Sky. "I could tell you things…."

Sky matched his defiant stare. "Bart has already told me everything."

Rowen's brows rose in mock suspicion. "Everything?"

Sky nodded, then winked at Bart. "All my life, I've wanted to say this. Rowen," she said, eyes on the tycoon, "this town ain't big enough for the both of us."

After a moment of stunned silence, Chet and Bart laughed, and the three of them watched Mike Rowen pick up his leather suitcase and leave his fancy hotel suite for the last time.

twenty

Sally jumped up and down, clapping her hands. "Oh, goodie. Oh, boy!" Lucy put her thumb and forefinger between her teeth and cut loose with a ripping loud whistle. Bud's double chins became three. And the Ice Lady gave a stare that put her other frigid looks to shame.

Chet stood in front of the elaborately carved marble fireplace, his arm protectively encircling Sky's waist. "We want a spring wedding," he announced.

Bud cleared his throat. "Well, I guess worse things have happened 'round here."

Sky had never been more terrified or nervous in her life. She stood before Stella Houghton, quaking from head to toe. Not that she expected her blessing. Even as a kid, Sky had never been a favorite of Stella's.

The woman rose slowly from her chair and moved toward her. "I suppose if you've made up your mind," she said to Chet, "there's no changing it." Then, shifting that breezy expression to Sky, she added, "He can be a very stubborn and determined man, you know."

Absent-mindedly, Stella smoothed Chet's collar. "We'll need to make proper arrangements, because no son of mine…." She cleared her throat. "No *son-in-law* of mine is going to be married under anything less than perfect conditions."

So Dale had been right, Sky realized. Stella loved Chet like her own flesh and blood and, though she'd never admit it, was afraid Sky might take him and Sally away from Four Aces…and her…forever.

"He's got a stubborn streak all right." Sky glanced up at him and smiled. "But he deserves only the best in spite of it." She met Stella's chilly gaze with one of warmth and sincerity. "I hope you'll remind me of that, in case I ever forget it." Sky hoped her little speech would tell Stella she'd always be a welcomed part of their lives.

Stella blinked, then looked at Chet. "Have you chosen a date?"

"We thought we'd leave that up to you," he said, a hand on her shoulder.

Bud joined them. "What's a guy gotta do to get a little attention around here?" He grinned, his chubby face pinker than usual, and held out his hand.

Instead of taking it, Sky gave him a big hug and kissed his cheek. Then, facing Stella, she held out her hand. "Friends?"

Stella's eyes misted as she put her hand into Sky's. The Ice Lady was melting and, beneath the hard surface, Sky saw what Chet had seen all along.

Sally danced around the room. "This is the best surprise ever," she said, hugging Chet's knees. "I love you, Daddy!"

He lifted her high in the air. "And I love you, sweetie." Sally kissed his cheek. Then, looking at Sky, she said, "Can I call you 'Mommy' after we get married?"

Sky's heart swelled with pride and love. "Of course you can, little one." She was suddenly aware of Bud and Stella, huddled together not three feet away. Sky looked to Stella for confirmation and approval.

The woman straightened her shoulders and smiled thinly. "Sally's lucky to have someone like you become a permanent part of her life." She lifted her chin after she said it, as if the stance was proof that her words were practical and realistic, and not simply rooted in sentiment.

Sky's dark eyes filled with tears. "And I'm lucky," she

said, "to be gaining two wonderful mothers after spending a lifetime without even one."

The women exchanged damp glances.

"Oh, get it over with, you bunch of softies," Bud said, pushing them into a group hug.

❧

As the weeks flew by, Sky barely had time to think about her cubs, let alone miss them. In her mind, they'd always be her cubs, though they were nearly full grown when she set them free on Beartooth Plateau.

For weeks before their release, she and Joe had been taking them up there, letting them hunt and reacquaint themselves with the wilderness. It was during that time that they'd been accepted as members of the wolf pack she'd been hearing while on their jaunts.

She'd found it impossible to say goodbye and had set up camp on Bit o' Heaven. And Chet, concerned when she didn't return after three days as she'd promised, had set out to find her. Sky would always remember the look of awe and respect on his face when he'd found her, frolicking on a bed of new-fallen snow with her cubs as the rest of the wolf pack watched, smiling their canine grins.

"I've gone and fallen in love with the wolf lady," he'd said.

The only sadness that had touched her life in the weeks since she and Chet broke the news of their wedding had been Bart's announcement that he'd be selling the Lazy L and moving out east. "Can't face you after what I did," he told her.

"Can't face you," Chet corrected once Bart was gone, "because he *loves* you."

Stella had completely taken over planning the wedding. Sally had already started calling her "Mommy." And traitorous Face had decided she was Sally's dog.

Life couldn't have been more perfect…until Stella took Sky

into her closet after one of their planning sessions. "Ella was too short to ever wear this," she said, unboxing an ivory satin gown, "but it should fit you perfectly."

Sky touched the soft, billowing folds. Holding it against her, she pirouetted in front of the mirror. Behind the high, lacy collar, edged with tiny pearl buttons, she felt like a Victorian princess. "It's beautiful, but...."

"I wore that dress thirty-five years ago. Something told me if I held onto it long enough...." Tears choked off her words.

"I know I'm a ghastly stand-in for Ella; she was so feminine and delicate, and I was such a klutz," Sky said, her own eyes swimming, "but I'll try to make you proud."

Stella squeezed Sky's hand. "You mustn't ridicule yourself. It's very unbecoming," she scolded gently. The Ice Lady had melted, all right, without leaving so much as a pool of cool water to remember her by. "You'll be a beautiful bride. You'll see."

epilogue

On a bright April morning, Sky studied her reflection in Gran's oval mirror. The chain from Wade's silver dog tags symbolized something old. The shiny good luck penny in her shoe was Dale's idea of something new. Lucy's cameo was something borrowed. And Joe's gift, a scrap of blue cloth from the cubs' blanket, tucked into her white rose bouquet, was something blue.

The dress fit as though it had been designed especially for her. Sky felt beautiful and ladylike—every bit that Victorian princess—as she swished into the waiting white limousine.

Residents of Mountain Gate packed the tiny log cabin church in the center of town as Sally and Face marched down the aisle to Martha's off-key piano rendition of "Here Comes the Bride." In the vestibule, Joe linked his arm with Sky's, and led her slowly toward the altar.

"'Behold, we call those happy which endure,'" Chet had quoted to her from James 5:11 that night in Rowen's parking lot, just before he'd slipped the engagement ring on her finger.

"'He who trusts in the Lord is happy,'" she'd answered.

When Chet lifted her veil, she broke with tradition just long enough to whisper her new life's motto into his ear: "Nothing ventured, everything lost."

He smiled and his left brow arched high. Sky didn't answer his unasked question. "We have a lifetime to learn the details," she reminded him. "A lifetime...."

A Letter To Our Readers

Dear Reader:

In order that we might better contribute to your reading enjoyment, we would appreciate your taking a few minutes to respond to the following questions. When completed, please return to the following:

Rebecca Germany, Editor
Heartsong Presents
P.O. Box 719
Uhrichsville, Ohio 44683

1. Did you enjoy reading *Montana Sky*?
   ❏ Very much. I would like to see more books by this author!
   ❏ Moderately
   I would have enjoyed it more if _____

   _____

2. Are you a member of **Heartsong Presents**? ❏Yes ❏No
   If no, where did you purchase this book? _____

   _____

3. What influenced your decision to purchase this book? (Check those that apply.)

   ❏ Cover   ❏ Back cover copy

   ❏ Title   ❏ Friends

   ❏ Publicity   ❏ Other_____

4. How would you rate, on a scale from 1 (poor) to 5 (superior), the cover design? _____

5. On a scale from 1 (poor) to 10 (superior), please rate the following elements.

    ___Heroine   ___Plot

    ___Hero   ___Inspirational theme

    ___Setting   ___Secondary characters

6. What settings would you like to see covered in **Heartsong Presents** books?_____

_____

_____

7. What are some inspirational themes you would like to see treated in future books?_____

_____

_____

8. Would you be interested in reading other **Heartsong Presents** titles?   ❑ Yes   ❑ No

9. Please check your age range:
   ❑ Under 18   ❑ 18-24   ❑ 25-34
   ❑ 35-45   ❑ 46-55   ❑ Over 55

10. How many hours per week do you read? _____

Name _____

Occupation _____

Address _____

City_____ State_____ Zip _____

Loree Lough

___*Pocketful of Love*—Out of their sorrow a friendship develops, and the possibility of love. However, vengeful enemies and jealous rivals determine to destroy the bloom of happiness Elice and Cabot have found in each other's arms. HP86 $2.95

___*Follow the Leader*—Everything Valerie held dear has been ruthlessly vanquished by the Civil War. Will a young widower with three children be God's instrument to free Valerie from the bonds of bitterness? HP154 (historical) $2.95

___*Pocketful of Promises*—Before joyous wedding bells will peal for Cabot and Elice, Cabot, a former cop, must go home again. Will Cabot forever put asunder his troubling emotions? HP157 $2.95

___*Montana Sky*—Lives planned without room for love are often interrupted by God's benevolent hand. When Sky and Chet find themselves participants in a wolf war, more than gunpowder is ignited. HP161 $2.95

___*Priscilla Hires a Husband*—To Priscilla and Caleb, a marriage of convenience seems the only solution. She'll do anything to provide for her beloved grandparents; he needs her help to rescue his failing farm. HP167 (historical) $2.95

········ Presents ········

Great Inspirational Romance at a Great Price!

Heartsong Presents books are inspirational romances in contemporary and historical settings, designed to give you an enjoyable, spirit-lifting reading experience. You can choose from 164 wonderfully written titles from some of today's best authors like Veda Boyd Jones, Yvonne Lehman, Tracie J. Peterson, and many others.

When ordering quantities less than twelve, above titles are $2.95 each.